SE JAKES

RUNNING ON EMPTY

A HAVOC NOVEL

RIPTIDE
PUBLISHING

Riptide Publishing
PO Box 1537
Burnsville, NC 28714
www.riptidepublishing.com

Running on Empty

Cover art: L.C. Chase, lcchase.com/design-portfolio.html
Editor: May Peterson
Layout: L.C. Chase, lcchase.com

ISBN: 978-1-62649-881-5

First edition
April, 2019

Also available in ebook:
ISBN: 978-1-62649-880-8

SE JAKES

RUNNING ON EMPTY

A HAVOC NOVEL

RIPTIDE
PUBLISHING

TABLE OF CONTENTS

PROLOGUE

WHAT YOU DO TO SURVIVE

Four months earlier . . .

When members of the Heathens Motorcycle Club first shoved Linc into the cell in the basement of their clubhouse, he'd asked, "Why?"

"You're our gift to Havoc." Bones smiled, and Linc resisted the urge to lunge at him, because it would only rip his arms out of their sockets. He'd already tested the mettle of the chains.

He could pop the cuffs, but he was surrounded. So he was biding his time, trying not to go fuck-nut crazy and hoping that sooner or later, members of Havoc MC—or at least his best friend, Rush, or his brother, Bram—would figure out where the fuck he was.

Or maybe Mercy. Mercy, a Havoc MC member, bail bondsman and the man Linc was currently sleeping with. But Mercy probably thought he'd flaked and run—that was his rep, after all, and he'd never tried to change it. Couldn't. Also, he'd never wanted to stay anywhere the way he wanted to stay at Havoc.

The longer he was kept in the basement, the more he overheard. First it was just "Geoff" and then, "He's Mercy now—what the fuck is that?" and then "This'll teach him." And over time, he was sure he'd convince himself a hundred times that he didn't hear anything.

He knew what Mercy's weight felt like on him, what the man's tongue did to him, but he'd never known Mercy's real first name. Mercy had never offered to share. Linc never pushed. When he'd been with Mercy, all he'd seen was a man who had his shit together. He'd never learned more about Mercy's troubled past . . . it was only now he learned that, somehow, it was tied to his own kidnapping by the Heathens.

What Linc did know—he'd gone out on his bike, the one he'd been restoring with help from some of the Havoc guys, and he hadn't planned on going far, but it'd been a nice night for a ride and he'd gotten caught up with the feel of the bike under him. Mercy was working out of town and Linc hadn't needed to rush back.

He'd never felt the need to rush anywhere, so to think about Mercy like that was definitely weird for him.

And that's when he'd gotten the call . . . and that's the point when everything changed. Instead of turning around and heading back to Shades without stopping, he'd pulled into the closest gas station to stop for a piss and a drink. He'd thought about texting Mercy to explain but he couldn't. Instead, he'd texted him a picture of the sunset, which was ridiculous and sappy but fuck it, Linc had never held back shit. Couldn't start now just because he'd started to . . . like . . . Mercy.

Yeah, *like*. That's as much as he'd been willing to say. Plus, he still owed the guy bond. And he'd gone over the state line, but hell, he was coming back.

At least that'd been the plan. Getting jumped by asshole Heathens definitely hadn't been. And even though Linc had fought, the shit they'd pumped him full of took effect before he could get in many punches. He did break a couple of noses though, he'd been told later as they kicked the shit out of him while he was still too numb to give a damn.

Now, with not so much as a goddamned Advil for two days, he gave a shit. After thirty-seven days, he was used to the pattern. They'd drug him up, beat him, torture him, and then nothing, because they wanted to watch him detox from whatever strong painkillers they were giving him to keep him pliant. And his body did, but not in a way that satisfied them.

Linc didn't want to disappoint them, but hell, he was never the one with the addictive personality. That was more his brother Bram's thing, and Bram was careful to not expose himself to shit like that. Linc liked pot and booze and feeling mellow, but he'd lived without it for long stretches of time—in the Army, when he was broke, when he felt he needed to make changes.

He'd kept track of how long the Heathens had kept him prisoner in their compound, by marking the cement of the cell floor, happy with himself that he was still semi-sane. They fed him, but half the time the shit was drugged too, and Linc was fucked enough without drugs. They'd never sat well in his system, which meant he slept a lot, which meant his whole keeping-track-of-the-days thing could be slightly off.

And, in between drugging him with whatever they got their hands on and Linc being alternately passed out and beaten, Bones would sit with him and tell him that he was Mercy's brother, that he'd killed one of Mercy's lovers before . . . and that there was a grave dug for him already, right next to Mercy's first lover.

But that hadn't been the worst of it, not by a long shot. Because Bones would detail exactly how that first lover had been killed. Excruciatingly vivid detail. And then he'd taken Linc on a field trip— not once, but several times—to the graves. He'd even threatened to make Linc climb into his, to make sure it fit.

In Linc's mind, that was the worst thing they'd done to him, but it definitely hadn't been the only form of torture. For men who hated fags, they sure hadn't minded fucking him. When Linc had pointed that out, he'd gotten beaten for his efforts but hey, he hadn't been there to make friends.

He'd never thought the POW training he'd gotten in the military would come in so handy in civilian life. Or that the training Castle had insisted he go through would be what got him through this hell.

But something different was happening now. He heard loud voices—Bones yelling at someone. Typically, they kept it quiet down here, because that added to the atmosphere of never knowing what would happen and when it would happen.

Something always did, though. Half the time he was too zoned out to care what the fuck they did to him. He kept his mouth shut and took what they gave him.

Today though, he refused to let himself ignore the yelling.

Today, for the first time in thirty-seven days, he had hope.

CHAPTER 1

DROP ALL YOUR TROUBLES
BY THE RIVERSIDE

After his rescue, Linc stayed in the hospital just under two weeks. He'd been too restless to just *sit around and get well*, and so, with his doctor's help—and Bram's—he'd moved into a lake house to finish his recovery and figure out his next steps.

He'd also had help from another source, but no one knew about that, and if Linc had his way, no one would.

The house Linc had insisted Bram rent was old and rambling, the kind of light, airy house he'd always wished they'd lived in growing up. Even as a kid, all he remembered was dark, damp walls closing in . . . although Bram and their sister, Linnea, always got him through the darkness. But the lake? Bram had shitty memories of growing up in houses on the water, but for Linc, they brought the same amount of comfort that being with Bram did.

Bram thought Linc didn't remember much about his near-drowning in another lake, another lifetime ago, by his father's hand. Bram was wrong, but Linc didn't see the purpose of dwelling on it or letting it change him. He brushed off the bad, focused on the good. The *what's next?*

He just kept it moving.

Of course, there were problems inherent with that too.

"I could live here," Bram said now, lying on his belly on the dock, propped on his elbows.

"You kind of are," Linc told him, the sun beating down on his chest, warming him as he lay next to his brother, his body worn out in a pleasant way from his most recent swim.

"Smart-ass. You know what I mean."

5

Yeah, he did. "Sweet misses you when you're here." Sweet being Havoc MC's president, and his brother's boyfriend. During Linc's recovery, he'd watched Sweet attempt to push Bram away. Bram, of course, wasn't one to be told what to do, and so Linc just looked upon their grand gestures as entertainment while he healed, happy to see that love did exist.

Bram and Sweet were firmly together now, evidenced by the fact that Sweet often spent the night here with Bram. And Linc was cool with that—his best friend, Sean Rush—and Rush's boyfriend and Havoc's XO, Ryker—stayed here together too. He was just happy for the company of people he was comfortable with.

Sometimes Tug would hang, and sometimes Boomer. Lately, Linc was able to stay here alone, although he knew someone from Havoc was always standing guard somewhere on the property.

He couldn't be babysat forever. He had to get on with his life, get his shit together. And he was, because he also managed to not think about or ask about Mercy for several hours at a time each day. And it was a major accomplishment, considering he'd mainly thought about Mercy the entire incarceration. Of course, Mercy felt too guilty to come anywhere near him, and Linc let him off the hook by telling Bram he didn't want to see Mercy and then banning him all together. Because everyone needed their lies to insulate them from the truth.

For the first several weeks, Linc couldn't remember much about what happened. Being kept prisoner at the hands of the Heathens filtered through first, usually while he slept, which resulted in screaming nightmares. And then he recalled the day of his actual rescue. Every day, more detail filled out, and he forced himself to go over it as much as possible, because remembering meant getting stronger.

Now, he closed his eyes and turned his face toward the sun, letting the memories drift in . . .

He'd smelled the fire before the smoke had billowed into the basement, and then he'd blinked and Mercy was walking through the haze, tossing him the keys to his cuffs before slamming Bones against the cement wall.

Mercy had lit the goddamned place on fire.

"You go, Linc. Go now," Mercy ordered him, and Linc knew that tone . . . and knew he was right. The smoke was thick and he'd unlocked his bonds, ignoring the urge to stay and watch Mercy beat the ever-loving shit out of Bones, and instead he navigated the dark hallways to get to the stairs. To get the hell out of here and into daylight. And he'd almost made it when Bruno came around the corner.

Thankfully, the keys hadn't been the only thing Mercy had thrown at him. Now, Linc's hands steadied as he drove the knife into Bruno's neck, the way he'd been taught, the way he'd done a time or two before, what seemed like a lifetime ago.

With Bruno's blood on his hands, Linc stepped out into the light, and into chaos. He stayed behind the tree line and made his way up the long drive toward the road, when he saw Bram's truck come barreling down in a cloud of dust. Heathens were starting to gather, to look for someone to fight, someone to blame in a last-ditch effort. Bram stopped the truck when he saw Linc, and Linc yelled at him to stay put and ran to him. He recalled throwing himself into the back seat and lying down, feeling the lurch of the vehicle and hearing Bram say he wasn't leaving his side.

The next minute, he was awake, in the hospital, and yes, Bram was there and Linc's mind was fuzzy. He was shaking, coming down from being injected daily with drugs, and his ribs ached like hell every time he tried to breathe. But he was free.

It was hard to think about those first days post-capture—post-rescue—when he'd barely been able to move. When he'd refused to see Mercy, and told Misha and Bram and Rush that he wanted Mercy permanently barred from his room . . . and that was after he'd learned that Mercy had assumed he'd run . . . that Mercy hadn't bothered to look for him, not until Bram had come to town.

He'd forced Bram to tell him, and his brother had done so—haltingly and reluctantly, as if not wanting to break Linc's heart but knowing that lying wasn't an option.

"He didn't know, Linc. I know he's hurting." Bram had tried to soften all the blows, but it hadn't helped.

"I don't want to see him, okay?"

"Not now, I get it."

"Not now. Not when I get out. Understood?"

"Yes."

And Bram had kept to his word. It hadn't been hard to do because Mercy never showed, never called, never tried, which in turn made Linc angrier. Which was good, because angry was better than numb any day, and Linc never wanted to be numb again. He'd spent thirty-plus days in that state, and he didn't need any reminders.

But he'd called Mercy at one point, at his weakest. After a nightmare that'd rocked him, he'd dialed Mercy's number and practically begged the man to call him back. And then he'd waited around like a lovesick asshole for Mercy to call him back.

He was still waiting.

He'd thought, somehow, that Mercy would've been his refuge. Instead, that's what the house became. He didn't tell Bram how he'd discovered it, and eventually, Bram would realize that his rent checks on the place weren't getting cashed, but for the next months post-capture, this house and the water would heal him better than any hospital ever could.

He'd have to take himself the rest of the way.

CHAPTER 2

IT DON'T COME EASY

I t took Mercy three weeks after taking down most of the Heathens' compound to decide that enough was enough, that being angry wasn't helping anything. So he got up and stopped mourning what was and he went back to his brothers.

Only Sweet and Tug knew that Mercy actually had left his house during those first weeks during his self-imposed house arrest. Every night, he'd snuck out of Havoc and headed to the hospital where Linc was, even though Linc had banned him from visiting, and he'd hold the watch in the hallway outside his door. It was the time that Linc most often had his nightmares, and Mercy knew he had to be there. Had to hear the screams, let them slice through him.

It was during those sleepless nights that he'd made decisions about his future. And once he'd made up his mind, there was no turning back. So after Linc had moved into the lake house, Mercy's first stop was to Sweet, and he hadn't needed to say much except, "I'd like to come back," to which Sweet replied, "I didn't think you'd ever left," and just like that, Mercy prepared to slip back into the day-to-day world of Havoc.

But first, there would have to be some changes. Because between the Heathens MC attempting to regroup and their friends, the Pagans MC, vowing vengeance, there was another MC called Project X attempting to patch over the remaining Heathens and start a new chapter near Shades Run. Now more than ever, Havoc needed to keep the drugs and the white supremacists out of their area.

"The bonds shop's not going to cut it anymore," Mercy told Sweet in a graveled voice, two days after making appearances in the clubhouse and in church.

Now Sweet told him, with zero hesitation, "Just tell me what you need."

"I need a more active role." Sweet would understand why and why *now*. Before this, the bonds shop had been perfect—it gave Mercy the necessary insulation to keep his identity safe.

Now, there was no reason to bother. He'd grown up son of the Heathens MC president. He knew how to handle himself. He'd proven that at a young age, and again when he killed his brother months earlier after he'd kidnapped Linc in an attempt to draw Mercy out. He knew how to defend, and how and when to kill.

"Enforcer?" Sweet asked. "I know Tug would be happy with the help. You've got seniority so . . ."

"I'm not looking to take anyone's job. I might have seniority but they've both been in their jobs for a while, and they're jobs I never held. So it's not about that."

"And the shop?"

Mercy looked at him. "I've put some thought into that. I don't know if having it in town works anymore. Maybe we need to move it closer to Havoc. But I'll get back to you on that."

Church had been called shortly after and many other decisions were made, including a lockdown of Havoc. Vann, a rogue Havoc member, would be called back into the compound indefinitely, and with that, the club officially circled the wagons.

Mercy was welcomed back by all his brothers in Havoc, some more subtly than others. Tug, of course, had picked him up and hugged him for what seemed like forever, and when he'd finally put Mercy down, he'd said, "Fuck the Heathens. You showed them. You're one of us."

And Mercy agreed.

His second-to-last stop had been to Bram, the man he'd fought with and then fought alongside of . . . the man whose brother he'd almost destroyed with his secrets. Linc and Bram were on the outside (Linc's choice, and Bram wouldn't leave him alone) and Havoc men were patrolling their lake house, guarding them. Bram was armed but Sweet was worried.

"How could you have known?" Bram asked. He looked better than he had when he'd first come into their lives. He'd gotten off most of the painkillers he'd been using because of his near-death beating at the hands of the Heathens. He hadn't quit the ATF yet, but his cover remained in place, among most of Havoc and with the Heathens and beyond.

"I should've. I got—"

"No, you didn't get complacent," Bram corrected before he could even say the word. "You were with your family. The Heathens? You never belonged with them."

"I don't know what to do . . . about Linc."

"Yeah, me neither," Bram confessed. "I just walk on eggshells around him and he does the same for me."

"I don't think he'll see me."

"Should that stop you from trying?" Bram smiled.

And his last stop? Would be a face-to-face that was long overdue.

CHAPTER 3

HOW DOES IT FEEL TO BE ON YOUR OWN

Linc woke from the nightmare with a sharp yell. It happened every single night like this, and he shouldn't have been surprised but he still was, even after nearly sixty straight days of this shit. He'd been hoping that maybe the universe would grant him a reprieve after the first thirty-seven days. The logical side, the one that had gotten him through basic training and beyond, told him it didn't work like that.

He wasn't sure if it was the doorbell that'd yanked him out of the dream, but he wasn't exactly in the mood to see anyone. Bram had a key, and so did Rush. So he went to the bathroom and took a piss, washed up, running his hands through his hair. It was longer than it had been, blonder too, from all the time spent in the sun, swimming in the lake.

The bruises had faded, along with DTs. The pain hadn't.

Whoever was at the door had taken to slamming on it like it was their mission to break in. Fuck. Linc grabbed his piece and headed to the door, opened it fast, and held his weapon out.

Mercy was on the other side, just staring at him . . . not looking surprised at all to see Linc with a gun. "I didn't mean to scare you."

Mercy. It was like seeing a ghost and *fuck*, his voice went down Linc's spine. It was raspy. Smoky. Hot as fuck and this was exactly why he hadn't wanted to see Mercy. It was bad enough that Mercy knew what the Heathens had done to him—if not outright, then he definitely suspected. Bram had learned it from the docs who took care of Linc in the hospital and Linc? Well, he'd lived it, every humiliating, brutal moment of it. Sometimes he'd begged, even though he'd been too drugged to know what he'd been begging for.

And he'd endured all of that for a man who hadn't made a move to see him since he'd escaped. Linc was sure Mercy had guilt, that seeing Linc reminded him of a fuckup. Now, Linc would always remind him of his past, and it was a past Mercy had tried for years to forget.

"What do you want?" Linc finally asked, his voice sounding rough, part under-use and part from near strangulation.

Mercy continued to stare at him, and Linc wanted to punch him. Linc knew he wasn't the same man he'd been the last time they'd seen each other, and he never would be. And after two months, Mercy was just fucking standing there . . . and the last time Linc had seen him, he'd been stalking through Heathens, slaying all Linc's dragons.

Mercy finally said, "I know you wanted me to stay away, but we need to talk."

How the fuck would you know what I really wanted? Linc shook his head no, anger mixed with shame bubbling up inside of him where neither emotion had existed before. He'd never had to be the angry, scared kid. Bram had always taken care of him, protected him, shielded him from the bad shit by making sure Linc was surrounded by amazing memories.

But his memories of recent events shattered any pretense, remained front and center, and no matter how hard Bram tried to help, it wouldn't work.

So now, confronted by Mercy, Linc's mind was conflicted more than ever. Technically, none of it was Mercy's fault.

Technically, all of it was.

The nightmare he'd woken from before the doorbell rang still shook him. He put the gun down on the table by the door and shoved his hands into his pockets so Mercy wouldn't see the tremble that he hoped would leave soon.

The dreams? They'd take much longer.

"I can't do this," Linc finally managed. "You're absolved, okay? I'm sure that's what you're looking for."

Mercy's back went up when Linc said that. He wanted to take Linc's face in his hands, force Linc to look at him, but he kept his hands to himself. "It's not about my conscience."

At that, Linc finally met his gaze as if to silently say *bullshit*.

There was so much Linc didn't know, and that was on Mercy. Because Mercy had chosen not to share that part of his life with anyone, except Sweet, and even Sweet didn't know the entire truth.

"I don't deserve your time. I know that. But Linc, fuck, I hate that you're suffering."

"So this is about me." Linc's voice was graveled, not the easy drawl Mercy had longed for every fucking night since Linc had gone missing. Every single night since Linc had been found.

And those months in between? Linc had suffered. Been to hell and back and Mercy was sure there was way more that had happened to Linc during his capture by the Heathens than anyone knew.

Everyone but Mercy, because he fucking knew . . . and that broke his fucking heart. "It's only about you."

"What makes you think I'd want to talk to you about anything?" Linc challenged, the haunted look in his eyes burned into Mercy's mind.

He'd snuck into the hospital, and he'd watched Linc sleeping, tubes running in and out of him. He'd wanted to rip the blankets off Linc, check his body for scars, kiss away all the pain and hurt he'd endured. "Because you used to talk to me about things. Things you never told anyone."

Linc didn't argue. "That was a long time ago."

"Not that long."

"So you want to be my shrink now?" Linc asked carefully. "What do you really want?"

You to be better. You not to have gone through this.

You. "I'm sorry, Linc. Fuck, I'd give anything for that not to have happened to you. Anything. I'd have taken your place in a second."

"Sure. Okay." Linc nodded with a wave of his hand. "You're absolved. Better?"

"That's not—fuck."

"Go away, Mercy. Go away and stay away. Clear enough?"

"Very. Except I'm not going to do what you're asking."

Linc turned away from him and Mercy forced himself to walk away, but not before telling him, "I'll be back."

"How comforting," Linc muttered, then slammed the door behind him.

CHAPTER 4

ONCE BITTEN, TWICE SHY

True to his word, Mercy was back at Linc's the next day. He knew that Bram split his time between Havoc and the lake house, but Bram had also told Sweet that Linc wanted to spend time alone, didn't want to be too scared to be by himself. And yes, the immediate threat had passed, but hell, the Heathens were going to remain a threat to anyone attached to Havoc, which necessitated extra protection for all Havoc members and their families.

Whether or not Linc knew that there was a protection detail attached to him at all times, Mercy had no idea. But so far, Linc had mainly stayed close to the house, only straying as far as the lake to swim.

Today, Tug was on duty, staying a respectable distance from the house, and tonight, Rush would come and stay over with Linc. They'd been best friends since boot camp, and even with that, Mercy knew Ryker would be waiting outside all night, watching over the men.

But it should be you, and not outside, either.

Then again, Linc hadn't realized Mercy was spending the night on his porch either.

Finally, Mercy pushed himself toward the backyard. Like he did every day, according to the other Havoc men who'd been on guard duty, Linc was swimming—back and forth across the length of the lake. Mercy counted twenty before Linc lifted his head, a subtle acknowledgment of his presence.

He didn't doubt Linc had known he was here the whole time, situational awareness, which bothered the fuck out of him. Because how the hell had Linc missed the Heathens closing in around him on the day he'd been taken?

Yeah, blame the victim, Mercy. But it wasn't that. He just desperately wanted things to have gone a different way.

Wanted Linc to have never crossed state lines. Wanted him to have stayed close to Havoc, where Heathens wouldn't dare come close.

And you didn't even think to look for him, Mercy chided himself. Not until he'd gotten in touch with Linc's brother, Bram, who'd been undercover at the time—and recovering from a deadly near-beating from the Heathens MC. In an eerie twist, the Heathens had nearly killed one brother and then did their best to break the second, with no knowledge of their familial relationship.

It was taken care of so they never would. But none of them could stop the Heathens permanently, although Mercy would try his damned best to eradicate them from their roots, in the town he'd grown up in, where the Heathens had burgeoned into the meth-pushing MC they'd become.

Walking onto a Heathens' compound for the first time since he'd renounced them at sixteen had been like walking onto foreign soil. Finally, he'd done what he should've a long damned time ago. Now, he figured there were Heathens waiting in the wings to try to take up the mantle, but none of them were born-and-bred MC men, which would make it that much more difficult. Still, Mercy and Havoc would make sure that Heathens didn't rise from the ashes, stronger than they'd been.

Linc swam languidly back to the dock, not rushing, not wanting another run-in with Mercy. He'd contemplated swimming for hours just to avoid another face-to-face but he was still not at a hundred percent.

"Nowhere fucking near," he muttered, just before yanking his aching body up onto the dock. Swimming was the only thing these days that gave him peace of mind. In the water, nothing else mattered except keeping his body moving, like a shark. Move or die. Plus, he'd always believed water had healing properties that were damned near unmatched.

By the time he allowed himself to look up, Mercy was gone.

"Good," he said out loud, even though it felt anything but. Because, since Mercy's visit yesterday, Linc had been restless. Irritable. He'd made Bram go to Havoc to visit Sweet, because Bram had been fussing over him, and then he'd alternately paced and brooded the rest of the evening, thinking about their first time together.

It was the same night Mercy had posted his bond. Linc had gotten arrested for fighting outside of Bertha's and Rush had called in a favor to Mercy.

After an hour of sitting in a cell in the sheriff's office, Linc had looked up to see Mercy, in his Havoc rocker, at his cell door.

That had been the beginning of a roller-coaster ride that Linc had never wanted to get off. Because Mercy was insatiable, and had been Linc's match in every way. Linc's body thrummed for him. And now, dammit, he was hard as fuck, and stayed that way even after diving back into the chill of the lake. Instead of letting the memories drown him, he put his head down and swam and swam until he could barely breathe . . . and when he looked up again, Mercy was still gone.

Hours after Mercy left and Linc jerked off in the shower—twice—he was still restless as fuck. Before the sun went down, he decided to go back into the lake for another swim, hoping to tire himself out enough so he could sleep through his nightmares.

When he looked up halfway through his swim, he noted that this time, it was Castle who was waiting for him on the dock. Still, he didn't rush his swim, took his time finishing—because routine soothed him more than anything else these days—before making his way over to the man whose house he was taking advantage of.

Castle would be unperturbed at having to wait. His patience was endless, unlike Mercy's. The men were opposites in many ways, but it was apples and oranges, because Linc's relationship with Castle was past . . . in every way except his job.

Because of that, he'd visited Linc in the first several days of his hospitalization, and offered him a way out of the sterile environment.

"There are too many eyes and ears. There's a lake house—just say an old military friend offered it up."

"And you're that old military friend, aren't you?" Linc asked.

Castle's eyes were soft with memories. "I'm not going to let anything happen to you again."

"None of this is your fault."

"I brought you into it."

"I'm a big boy, remember?"

Castle shook his head, his lips pressed together, and Linc could see how angry he was about Linc's capture. "I remember everything, Linc."

"You want me back to work."

"I think you want yourself back. But let's get you healed up first and then we'll talk."

Linc was angry, dizzy, and fully unprepared. But fuck, if he ever wanted to work this way again, he had to protect the covers he'd cultivated. So he took the keys and the papers and told Bram about the house.

Bram was no fan of hospitals himself, and he was just as eager to get Linc to a more normal location to heal.

"Hey," Linc said now, hands on the dock.

"Hey yourself." Castle was sitting in one of the deck chairs, mirrored glasses on, looking handsome. "Glad you're making use of the lake."

Linc heaved himself out of the water. Every day, it became easier. He flopped into the chair next to Castle, letting the sun warm his body. The scars—the ones he hated the thought of showing Mercy— were on full display, and he noted Castle cataloging them.

"The house is awesome," he said, as a way of taking Castle's attention off them.

He didn't say thanks about the house, because it wasn't a favor. More like a barter. The FBI owed him, and this wasn't a bad form of payment. And the distraction hadn't stopped Castle from staring hard at his scars, his expression tight.

"I'm fine," Linc said quietly.

"You're strong," Castle agreed, then paused, his face serious. "I want you to rest assured that Matlin's been taken care of."

The last time Linc had seen his old handler was in Texas, when his family and friends thought he'd run again and his attitude about that had always come down to, *fuck it, there are worse things for family and friends to think about me . . .* until it came to bite him in the ass when he'd been captured and his handler had totally and utterly failed him.

Because a handler was supposed to keep track of their charge, and keep them safe, on and off their ops.

That failure had gotten Linc reassigned to Castle, who'd apparently thrown a fit when he'd learned what'd happened to Linc. Considering they used to hook up when Linc was in the Army, he supposed it was good to know the guy was still in his corner.

He also supposed it was more serious than just hooking up, especially after Castle left the Army for the FBI and there weren't rules against their relationship.

Castle had recruited Linc early in his Army career, after Linc had taken an E&E training seminar with him. Castle had been impressed enough with Linc's skills—and his other high scores—and had discussed the possibilities of black-ops jobs with him. His sleeping with Castle hadn't depended on the jobs—and vice versa—but for various reasons, they'd kept their relationship on the down-low.

"Are you thinking about getting back to it?"

Linc shrugged. "Guess it depends."

"On how much you can explain to Mercy?" he asked and Linc nodded. "I don't see him here, though."

"You just missed him." But he figured Castle knew that, probably waited for him to leave. "Don't bullshit me like this. Say what you came here to say."

"I know you've been through hell. I do. But I also know that just hanging out at Havoc isn't you. Just because you let people think it is."

Motorcycle clubs hadn't been on Linc's radar until he'd enlisted. Yeah, he'd known they existed, but until he'd been stationed near Shades Run, he hadn't realized that there were differences between the clubs, whether they were one percenters or not, and how many wars were waged between the MCs. Or that they'd originally started out in order to help returning veterans.

He'd learned, before Mercy, that Havoc was founded by four such vets by buying cursed land and making a go of it.

Later, Ryker confirmed it. "The land liked them. Still does, so it watches out for us."

After spending time on the compound, Linc could believe it. There was a good energy, a sense of peace and calm, no matter what was going on in the outside world.

But until Linc had served and gotten out, he hadn't understood the importance of being with like minds, with men and women who understood what he'd dealt with in the Army. The shit he'd seen.

It was why he'd been drawn to Jethro as well. Jethro and Castle were old friends, so Linc had known Jethro for years. Meeting him as a Hangman went down without a hitch because Linc also understood the world of covert ops.

Because Linc *was* that world. "You can't tell me I haven't been exposed."

"Listen, I'd have heard something by now. Heathens kept you hidden and by doing so, made it hell on you, but easy on your cover."

"Great. Glad the cover is more important than my fucking life."

"It's not, Linc." Castle looked remorseful, and Linc knew that he'd taken over being Linc's handler because of the screwup that'd kept him locked in the Heathens basement for months. But still, the bitterness seeped in at unexpected times. Especially when he thought he'd finally put it behind him.

He was beginning to realize there was really no such thing. "I need time," he repeated stubbornly.

"I won't argue with you. Stay here as long as you need to. I'll keep checking in."

"To see if I'm ready?"

"To make sure you're all right," Castle corrected.

CHAPTER 5

IF I CAN GET YOU TO SMILE
BEFORE I LEAVE

Now, more restless than ever and feeling the walls closing in on him, Linc called Rush to announce, "It's been a goddamned day. I need to get the fuck out of here."

Rush made a sympathetic grunt. "I'll come over. I'll bring pizza and beer and we'll hang by the lake."

"No. I need to go out."

"Want me to bring you here?"

Here meant *Havoc*. So *no*. Linc sighed and tried again. "Who's out there guarding me tonight?"

"Hang on—I stole the list off Ryker's phone."

"Of course you did." And he was never more grateful for Rush's pickpocketing ways. It helped to know who he'd be facing down while he broke out of his self-imposed jail.

"Shit—it's Vann."

Vann was talked about in hushed terms by the majority of the Havoc members. Rumor had it he was a contract killer, which was why he spent so much time on the road.

It made sense. "That's cool. So are you meeting me at Bertha's?"

Rush cursed under his breath. "Are you kidding me, Linc? How're you gonna get past Vann? Because you and I both know his rep."

"Yeah, he's crazy. At this point, I might be crazier, so we should get along just fine. You're closer, so you'll be there first."

"Wait, you're ready to go now?"

"Is that a problem?"

"It's only three in the afternoon."

"Close enough to happy hour for me," Linc countered. "Unless you're all whipped now. Soft and shit."

"You fucker," Rush snarled.

"See you soon." He hung up before giving Rush a chance to say no, dressed quickly, grabbed his wallet and his sunglasses, found his helmet by the front table, and went out to his bike. Bram had kept it up for him, with Linc's permission, because an unused hog was a goddamned crime.

Now, he stared at the gorgeous dark beast and wondered what was the worst that could happen on his first ride alone since he'd been taken—on another ride alone—by Heathens.

Well, if all goes well, you won't be alone. It's not like Vann wouldn't give chase, he reasoned.

Or he could have a major fucking panic attack and that would take care of his entire plan, fast. But okay, yeah, he could deal with that.

He sat on the steps, next to the bike and just breathed, because once he got on it, there was no pausing. He couldn't give Vann time to think. Linc had to be like a charging bull . . . except that Vann? Kind of like a bull-slash-matador—and a brick wall—all at once. The rumors about him weren't just rumors, according to Bram.

Worst worst case? Vann stopped him cold.

You've got to do it. Because if he couldn't even ride his bike on the open road, he had bigger problems than he thought.

He breathed in the cool night air and got on the bike and prepared for the open road.

Crazy Vann will at least follow you . . . if you can get past him.

Hell, Linc still loved a challenge. He booked it down the road, staring at the open space to Vann's left. Vann swung the bike right and Linc blew past him. And laughed.

He checked the mirror and saw Vann following him, not too close but not too far, either. So he settled in and let the open road soothe him, the bike humming between his legs, his muscles pleasantly sore from the work involved in keeping this beast on the road for an hour.

God, there was nothing fucking like it. Except sex.

Finally, and almost reluctantly, he pulled into the lot behind Bertha's. Vann pulled in right next to him, was off his bike before Linc was, standing there like a brick wall, and, for the first time, Linc questioned his own sanity.

Because even though he'd never met Vann in person, he'd seen the pictures on the clubhouse wall. And the stories? Legendary.

In person? The stories and the pictures didn't do him justice. Linc groaned silently and then mouthed off because he couldn't help himself. "Are you really going to try to babysit me tonight?"

He held his breath, but Vann grinned, and Linc swore that he could get pregnant from that smile.

Then Vann wiped his bottom lip with his thumb. "Sweetheart? I don't babysit anyone. If I didn't want to be here, I wouldn't be."

His voice was deep. Scary and sexy at the same time.

"So you let me go on purpose?" Linc asked.

"Looked like you needed to. Badly." Vann shrugged. "Riding's better than sitting around any day of the week. Was that guy who stopped by giving you trouble?"

"No." Linc shook his head. "It's complicated."

"What isn't?"

"Tonight. Drinking. Dancing. That's what I'm going to do."

"Over whose dead body?"

"I guess it'll have to be yours," Linc said wryly, enjoying the light flirting, mainly because Vann considered his words with a head tilt and a gleam in his eye. "Or you could just come inside with me and drink and dance. I'm sure there will be women there you can fool around with."

Vann studied him, his dark eyes like the goddamned devil's. And then his mouth broke open in a smile and yeah, a devil for sure. "Not looking to fool around with a *woman*." And the way he said it? *Yeah* . . . "So, Linc . . . let's go drinking and dancing."

He'd been so focused on getting inside that he hadn't realized how goddamned crowded it would be, even at four in the afternoon. Granted, far less than it would be in several hours, but still. And even though it was all friendly faces, the last time he'd been in a crowd this big . . .

Shit.

"You going to be okay?" Vann asked.

"Great. Fine," he answered absently, but Vann stepped in front of him for a brief second, forcing Linc to stare up at him.

"You don't go through what you did without scars. I'm just asking if I can help—arm on your back? Or will touching you freak you the fuck out? Shit like that."

Then Vann moved back by his side and Linc stared straight ahead, because if he didn't, he was afraid he'd chicken out. "Just . . . touch me. Okay?"

Vann put a hand on his back, held it there as they moved into the main doors and beyond.

And it wasn't weird. It was . . . comforting. Flirtatious. "Were you told . . . to treat me like . . ." He couldn't finish, mainly because he didn't want to know.

"No. I was told not to let your ass off the property. Not to entertain or enable you," Vann assured him gruffly. "I'm not a fucking people person, Linc. I'm the one they call when they need someone beat up or shit blown up, dig? Usually, I'm not fit for human company. So even if they ordered me to be nice to you, I would've done the opposite."

"So why did you agree to come with me?"

"You need to smile more." Which Linc did, briefly, at his words. "There's your boy."

Yes, Rush was already there, at one of the back tables, waiting. If the bartenders or the bouncers were surprised to see Linc, they hid it well. They were welcoming but not overly smothering, and he sat next to Rush and Vann sat on his other side.

Vann nodded at Rush. "You're Ryker's, yes?"

"Christ," Rush muttered, and Vann laughed and shook his head.

The music was low enough to have conversation. Food was being served, mostly bar stuff, and Vann ordered them a bunch for the table. A few Hangmen MC members came over to talk to him, and they nodded in Linc and Rush's direction, but kept their conversations focused on Vann.

Linc had fond memories of this bar. It was Havoc-owned, and he and Rush and Noah used to sneak in here during their days in the Army, even though they'd been prohibited from doing so. It was always a good time, a mix of regular people and MC members from Havoc and Hangmen and Vipers and the like. No Heathens or Pagans had ever been allowed in here, and from what Linc knew, they'd never even bothered to try.

When Rush started hanging out with Ryker—and Havoc—on a regular basis, they'd come here more frequently. This was where Linc had first seen Mercy, and then spent the next several months trying to get Mercy to actually notice him.

He'd gotten drunk and gotten arrested purposely to get Mercy's attention and that'd worked (although he'd never told anyone that had been his ultimate plan). So now, he reasoned, he'd broken out, would get drunk and try to get Mercy's attention that way (because he wasn't doing the get-arrested thing again, since he still had to go to court for the first arrest) . . . because insanity was doing the same thing twice and expecting different results . . . and he wasn't insane. He wanted the same damned results.

"You're thinking about Mercy again." Rush broke into his reverie. "You get this look in your eyes."

Linc didn't bother denying it. "It doesn't matter. He's not thinking about me at all, beyond making a protection schedule that doesn't include him. Except for today's unannounced visit." At his words, Rush shifted and looked guilty as anything, so Linc immediately accused him. "You knew he was coming."

"No . . . I mean, yes. Dammit." Rush did a shot, then blurted out, "He's been visiting you at night."

"Like Ryker visited you? Because I think I'd wake up screaming in an entirely different way."

Rush snorted. "Not like that. He just . . . waits. Stays up to make sure you're okay."

Listens to your screams. "Since when?"

The expression on Rush's face said it all, but he confirmed, "Since your first night in the hospital."

"But I banned him."

"Can't ban people from the hallway. Besides, Misha . . ."

"Right." Sweet's sister was an ER doctor and had watched over him for most of his stay in the hospital and again now, while he was at the lake house.

"Don't get pissed at him."

He wasn't angry, just confused. "So he visited me at the hospital. How long have you known about this?"

"I wasn't supposed to tell you," was Rush's nonanswer. "I thought it might freak you out. Plus, Ryker gave me strict instructions that I couldn't tell you, but hey, since you actually asked . . ."

Linc understood Rush's dilemma. And he got why Mercy wouldn't want him to know. After all, Linc was the one who'd banned Mercy from the hospital and the house, saying he didn't want to see him, so what did he expect? Obviously, Mercy staying here didn't mean anything beyond protection, which he no doubt felt bound to do, and he didn't want Linc to read into anything. "It's fine. Doesn't mean anything."

Rush just stared at him like he was an alien. "Now I understand why Noah wanted to kill me when Ryker started sending me roses and I blew it off and thought he was making fun of me."

"Well, that *was* dumb," Linc muttered.

"Right. *That* was dumb." Rush rolled his eyes. "Did you not hear me? Mercy slept at the hospital every single night. Watching over you."

"Because he didn't like being told what to do. Purely obstinate." Linc shrugged. "Obligation. Guilt."

"And he stays at the lake house too. Every night since you first got there. He sleeps out on the porch, rain or shine."

Dammit. "I need tequila."

Rush paled visibly. "No, not the tequila. That's full of bad decisions and recriminations."

"Yes," Linc said firmly. "You and me both."

"As much as I'd like to affirm your bad judgment, who will drive me home then?"

"Fine. Then I'm drinking all of it," Linc told him, and he saw fear in his friend's eyes.

"God, we're *fucked.*"

At the mention of *fucked*, Vann perked up. "Come again?"

"Tequila," Linc repeated.

"I'm on it." Vann went to the bar.

"Why's he so nice to you?" Rush demanded.

"He's probably planning on blowing me up later," Linc surmised.

Vann snorted from behind him. He poured Linc a shot from the full tequila bottle he held. He'd also brought a salt shaker and a bowl of lemon wedges.

Linc wasn't taking anything stronger than Advil at this point, so he said fuck it and took the shot. And then a second and his brain calmed the fuck down.

"Great service." He toasted Vann.

Vann seemed amused by him.

He was probably that way right before he killed someone.

CHAPTER 6

SOMEBODY'S BABY

Over the course of the next hour, Vann continued to ply him with shots (and, to be fair, food and water). He was an outrageous flirt . . . and fuck it all, so was Boomer, who pulled his chair over and joined in the fun.

And then Linc was dancing—with Vann and Rush and Boomer and an entire crowd of people. For the first time in a long time, there was no pain. He was still all hollowed out inside, but for these moments, he was happy. The pound of the music blasted out the back of his skull, his skin warmed as Vann and Boomer's hard bodies hemmed him in. Rush was on the dance floor too, flirting with some of the women of Havoc. For some reason, Rush could get away with that shit where none of the other men could.

On one of his many dance floor breaks, Linc downed a couple of waters with a beer chaser, listening to Vann's stories and enjoying himself more than he had in a long time. He was still lonely, which was an odd fucking feeling for him, and the hole in his heart wasn't going to be filled that easily.

But hell, Vann was being a damned good friend.

Speaking of damned good friends, Rush suddenly turned to him, his face frozen in an *oh shit* expression and yelled over the music, "Tug's here."

Which really, wouldn't be that big of a deal, except Tug had his phone to his ear and was making a beeline straight toward them. He'd definitely been sent or called here.

"Hey guys." Tug stopped at their table and glanced at Vann, who gave him a nod and wink. "So, what's up?"

"How'd you know we were here?" Linc asked outright.

"Wasn't me," Vann told him.

"Me neither," Boomer echoed.

Linc glanced at Rush. "You were followed."

"He thought he was alone, if that helps," Tug offered, a small smile akin to that of a naughty child who was quite proud of his transgressions.

Rush glared at him. "I wasn't followed—"

"Not that you can tell."

"I know how to lose a tail, Tug," Rush insisted. "So what the hell?" And then a look of horror crossed his face. "Was some kind of chip implanted in me when I slept?"

"You watch too much of that Jason Bourne shit," Tug chided.

"With you," Rush pointed out and Tug laughed and Linc had to admit he'd missed this camaraderie.

"Has to be the car," he told his friend.

Rush shook his head. "I checked the car. Don't you think I know . . ." He froze. Looked down and glared at the watch he wore like it was the enemy.

Then he took it off, threw it on the ground, and smashed it under his boot. He reached down and scooped up the parts, sifted through and pulled out a bug. "That fucker had a tracker in his watch."

"That's Ryker's?" Linc asked.

"Yes, dammit," Rush said as Ryker magically appeared. "And you know better than to say his name out loud."

"So he's like a fuckin' genie now?" Vann asked, and Linc snorted in collusion.

Ryker, however, wasn't amused, standing there, arms crossed. The first thing Rush did was stand and grab Ryker's hand. He opened it and poured the pieces of the broken watch into his palm.

"That was my favorite watch," Ryker said mournfully, staring at the pile of metal and glass Rush had dumped into his palm.

"You get what you give."

"Wearing it that first night," Ryker said, and Rush's expression softened. "'S'all right, baby. You're more important than any watch."

An odd tug yanked at Linc's heart that he recognized made him turn away and subsequently ignore it.

At least Mercy hadn't come—it was better that way.

As if Vann sensed Linc's sudden change of mood, he passed him a shot and took one of his own, clinking their glasses together. Then Vann's arm went around his chair, like he was shielding him. "You don't have to leave till you're ready. No one's getting through me."

"You said you're not babysitting me."

"I'm not. But I know what happened. Just letting you know that I've got your back." He ran his knuckles along Linc's cheek and a sudden flare of desire burned in Linc's belly. It was the first time he'd actually felt it since his escape, and it was nice to know he was still capable of it.

He wished he could get Mercy off his mind, but the man next to him was a great diversion, and a hell of a good time. The old Linc would've already kissed him.

The new Linc? Still way too hesitant.

Boomer had his truck with him, and sometime after two in the morning, he loaded Linc and Vann's bikes inside and drove them back to the lake house.

Vann unloaded the bikes in the driveway, and Boomer drove away with a wave.

"Aren't you going back to Havoc?" Linc asked.

Vann shook his head. "I'm on duty till sun up."

"Want to come in?"

Vann smiled. "Ah, babe . . . yeah, I do. But I'll wait at the end of the drive, like I'm supposed to."

Fuck, it was nice to be wanted.

"Hey Linc? There's one thing you need to know—and maybe you do already. But when an MC man saves you . . . you're his. Until he's done with you. And Havoc men? They don't take that lightly. Mercy won't."

Linc let that swim around in his alcohol-addled brain and decided to pretend he hadn't heard it. "Thanks . . . for tonight. It helped."

"I'm glad." Vann turned to go.

"Vann?"

"Yeah?" Vann looked over his shoulder from his seat on the bike.

"Can we do it again?"

"Definitely."

"Tomorrow night?" Linc hedged.

Vann laughed—which Linc took as a yes—then raised a hand and roared the bike the half mile to the end of the drive, just outside the gate.

Linc stayed where he was for a long moment, the happy buzz still making him floaty. Then he remembered what Rush told him, about Mercy spending the night here.

Did Vann know that happened too?

Now, Linc stood and reached for the blanket that was always folded up on the porch chair. It smelled like Mercy, and for a long moment, he rubbed his face against it, then he folded it and left it there.

That night, he slept on the couch on the other side of the wall, with a hand pressed against the wall, because that was the closest he could get to Mercy.

Pathetic.

Flirting with Vann. Jerking off to Mercy. Spinning out of control. But if it got him closer to Mercy, closer to healing?

He'd fucking keep spinning.

CHAPTER 7

NO MORE MR. NICE GUY

Of course Mercy knew that Linc was sneaking out and heading to Bertha's. It was probably the worst kept secret ever, but hell, Linc seemed to be enjoying himself for the first time in a long time.

It worried Mercy that Linc was out and about—vulnerable—but he'd let that go, assuming that Linc would grow tired of going out on a nightly basis.

After four nights, he still hadn't.

And each and every one of those nights, Mercy wanted nothing more than to go to Bertha's in order to haul Linc's ass home and chain him someplace safe . . . like his bed.

But that would be ridiculous. Instead, he did his patrols and then he went to the lake house.

Tonight, the fifth night of Linc's merry evade and escape, Mercy had gotten the text that Linc was home, safe and sound, around two in the morning. Mercy arrived soon after, parked outside the gate of the lake house and headed to the porch—as usual. When he was maybe fifteen feet away, he saw Linc just standing on the porch. Mercy froze in place, although he was certain Linc knew he was out here.

Linc was already shirtless in the moonlight, sitting on the couch that Mercy slept on. Then he stood, lowered his sweats enough to free his cock and began to jerk himself off and damn, the boy looked fine. Gorgeous.

"You little son of a bitch," Mercy murmured with a smile. Because whatever Linc had gotten into tonight at Bertha's obviously hadn't tamped down his want of Mercy . . . and Mercy was grateful for that.

Mercy wanted to finish the job for him, push him down under that beautiful spill of moonlight and take him, fast, then slow, until they were both spent. Instead, he watched, his own cock a hard throb in his jeans as Linc spilled over this hand, shot up his chest and cried out loud enough so Mercy could hear it. And then Linc leveled his gaze up, as if meeting Mercy's eyes, and it literally took everything Mercy had not to go to him, to answer the call of the gorgeous taunt. To take him down in the soft moonlight.

But neither man was ready for that, as evidenced by the fact that, after several long moments, Linc turned and went inside, closing the door behind him. Linc's show would have to be enough for now.

Linc was crying out for his attention. Mercy was giving it to him, in the best way he could right now. Because it was too soon—much too soon—or so he thought. He hadn't known how to reach Linc, exactly, and the walls between them were so much more than symbolic.

It was time for Mercy to bring the walls down between them, to find out who the man visiting Linc was . . . and why Linc had known Jethro was undercover before Bram had. It might be as simple as Rush telling him so, but Mercy had other suspicions. There were missing pieces he was struggling to put together, on top of the soul-crushing guilt he bore at knowing another man in his life had gotten hurt because of him . . . and his association with the Heathens.

Yes, tomorrow, things were changing.

When Mercy got to church the next afternoon, Vann was waiting for him.

"Why aren't you taking care of him?" Vann demanded, with no preamble.

"Who?" Mercy asked, the anger building inside of him. He was already on edge after a mostly restless sleep that consisted of imagining Linc on the other side of the wall, and if that wasn't the perfect metaphor for what was happening between them, he didn't know what was.

Vann rolled his eyes. "You haven't touched him. And Linc needs to be touched."

Mercy grit his teeth. "We're not together."

"Because you refuse to fuck him."

"You have no idea—"

"I know what he went through. I know some might not need touching. But Linc? He needs it to feel whole. And if it's not going to be from you . . ."

"Then you'll step in?"

"I'd never do that to a club brother," Vann said seriously. "But he's going to find someone else. I'm just trying to keep him close."

Mercy leaned against the doorjamb. "I came here to talk about that with everyone. I've been giving him too much freedom."

"So you're not going to let him go out?"

"I didn't say that. But everyone needs to know that he's mine. And above all else, he needs to know that."

"I'm guessing you've got a plan."

For the first time in a long time, Mercy definitely did. And when he went inside and sat at the table with Sweet, Tug, Ryker, Boomer, and Vann, he announced with finality, "It's time to take Linc in hand."

"Thank Christ," Sweet muttered, and Mercy couldn't blame him. So far, in his five-day spree, Linc had managed to rope Vann, Tug, Boomer and, of course, Rush—and Noah and Casey—into his merry reign of terror crossed over with evade and escape. God might've created the world in seven days, but Linc was threatening to bring down two MCs in a far shorter timeframe, all with the help of tequila.

And no one was complaining, except Mercy.

And now, Sweet. Although he'd been smiling every time someone caught him up on Linc's escapades. Because *Linc*.

"It hasn't been *that* bad," Tug protested.

"You were singing 'I've Got You Babe' with Vann," Sweet pointed out.

"Vann took Cher's part," Tug protested, like that made it better.

Vann? Just smiled.

Mercy turned to Sweet. "How did you know about the singing?" Sweet's brows rose in feigned innocence and Tug failed to hide his laugh. "Christ, not you too."

"It's definitely time to circle the wagons," Sweet said definitively, forcing his expression serious. "Listen, I'm hearing chatter from the docks. Project X has been sniffing around."

Mercy had been the one to find out that particular bit of intel, just last night, so he all around agreed that time was of the essence.

After church business wrapped up, he stayed behind to clarify additional things with Sweet. "I've made some decisions about the shop. I'm thinking Linc should run it."

"Linc?"

Mercy looked at him, unblinking. "Yes."

"Shouldn't it be Linc's decision?"

"No. It should be yours. And mine." Mercy paused. "And the clause? I'm invoking it. In case 'taking him in hand' wasn't clear enough."

"Okay. Formally noted. It's well within your right," Sweet agreed. "Is there more?"

Yes, there was more. It was time for Mercy to get off his ass, once and for all, and make sure this never happened again. "One last thing . . . no more hiding."

Sweet narrowed his eyes. "Is that what you think you've been doing?"

"It was always a big game of chicken—I knew it and so did Bones. Lying that way made it impossible. What happened was only a matter of time. Everyone should've known who I was, and then they could've chosen whether they wanted to be a part of the danger I brought here."

"Putting it out there would've started a war, and one that would've had a hell of a lot of casualties. You know that. You made a hell of a sacrifice."

"I didn't sacrifice shit. Linc? He's the one who paid. Linc and David." Mercy shook his head. "It's out there now. I'll make it my life's work to dismantle the Heathens."

"No!" Sweet ordered. "You'll make it your life's work to defend and strengthen Havoc. Make sure no one touches our members and their families. You can't save the world, Mercy—you can only defend your piece of it. Your land, your people . . . and do no harm to those who don't harm you."

Mercy clenched his teeth. "I can do both, Sweet. You just watch me."

"At what cost to yourself?"

Mercy grunted in response and waved Sweet off from asking anything further. His mind was made up, and the first thing he'd do was to get Linc's ass into the Havoc compound . . . and keep him there.

CHAPTER 8

FOOLED AROUND AND
FELL IN LOVE

The nights out had allowed Linc to sleep better than he had in months. The nightmares were muted, and last night, it was simply a dream about Mercy that had him waking with his cock in hand, hard and unsatisfied.

A dream about their first time together . . . a memory that was imprinted on Linc so strongly that even amnesia wouldn't erase it.

The bar fight started innocently enough. Rush and Noah had been there with him at Bertha's and, of course, tequila had been along for the ride.

Tequila fueled his not-so-bad decision that night, when Mercy walked into Bertha's and then left after half an hour without making any sort of eye contact with him. And Linc had tried to get his attention. Tried like hell, and had succeeded in getting a lot of attention from everyone except the one person he'd been trying to attract.

He needed a more direct approach, and getting arrested so Mercy could post his bond seemed so logical. He didn't tell Rush or Noah his plan because he figured they wouldn't recognize genius when they heard it. Instead, he bumped into a couple of guys walking through the bar and then told them to fuck off because guys were so goddamned easy and testosterone-fueled to start with—add alcohol and pretty girls and they were more than eager to start throwing punches. Which was exactly what had happened.

Except Linc wiped the floor with them and then he'd fought the bouncers when they'd tried to help. Even Rush couldn't get them to not call the police, and his friend had tried. But Rush promised him that he'd get bail.

"Call Mercy—don't use your own money, man," Linc told him.

"That'll probably be faster," Rush agreed. "No matter what, I'll get you out."

The cops were decent to him, mainly because he'd calmed down as soon as they came, and he was respectful because it wasn't their fault. They were just doing their job, and he'd been chagrined.

He hadn't even used his phone call, because by the time he'd been booked and put in a cell, Mercy was there in person to free him.

And Linc? For the first time in his life, he'd felt slightly shy when the big man with the tattoos and easy-going attitude led him out of the station and toward his waiting SUV. He opened Linc's door for him, but Linc forced himself to shake off his shyness, and leaned in toward Mercy.

"Thanks for bailing me out."

"It's my job."

"Still, you didn't have to come all the way down here just for me. I know Rush called in a favor."

Mercy looked amused. "He did."

"Maybe I can make it worth your while."

"Yeah?" Mercy's brows rose. "How're you going to do that?"

Linc smiled, still slightly drunk and all too fucking happy for someone who'd been arrested. "We could take it out in trade."

"Do you have it in you?"

By then Linc had been running his finger along Mercy's chiseled biceps, tracing the Havoc logo he knew was hidden under the long-sleeved Henley. "More than."

"That's what they all say."

"Consider this my audition." Because Mercy's big, warm palm was touching his skin, and Linc wanted to kneel at the man's feet and do anything he ordered. His mind went blank, because Mercy chuckled and turned him around to face the car door . . .

And that's when Linc heard the clink of handcuffs behind him. Before he could say anything, Mercy had one of his arms behind his back and Linc felt the cold steel circle his wrist. "And here I thought I was a free man."

"You're not," Mercy murmured. "There's always a price to pay."

"So we're working it out in trade?"

Mercy tugged his other hand behind his back and Linc's hands were cuffed together. Mercy turned him and began unbuttoning his shirt, stroking along Linc's bare chest. "Yeah, we're gonna have some fun tonight."

He'd helped Linc into the SUV, driven to the bonds shop, and walked Linc upstairs to the apartment that was housed above it. Before Linc could say anything else, Mercy had stripped him, uncuffing his wrists for a moment to take his shirt completely off.

And then Mercy was kissing him—or maybe he'd leaned in to kiss Mercy first, but it didn't matter, because the kiss was explosive. Their tongues dueled for dominance, and he was all too happy to let Mercy win, because he was the best kisser Linc had ever known, and hell, he'd been kissed a lot.

Mercy grabbed his hair to hold him in place while he tongue-fucked his mouth, slid his hand down to Linc's ass and let his fingers play between Linc's ass cheeks as he groaned into Mercy's mouth.

Then Mercy was biting along his neck and shoulders, palming his cock, and Linc was mumbling about "wanting you naked and inside me now" and Mercy was laughing and finally—finally—Mercy had noticed him. Linc basked in the attention, because it was like being warmed by the sun. He ran his hands all over Mercy's chest and shoulders, smelling the leather he wore under his cut and trying to tug Mercy's clothing off, but Mercy told him, "You're not the one in control here."

"I'm okay with that."

"Good thing" was all Mercy said, and then Linc was once again bound, hands behind his back, his forehead pressed to the mattress, ass in the air.

"Is this what you expected tonight?" Mercy asked from behind him.

Linc bit his tongue because maybe expected wasn't the right word—hoped for, fantasized about, yes, but expected? No, he'd never thought the reality would actually be better than the fantasy.

When he'd first laid eyes on the blond-haired, tattooed biker, he'd known. There was something about the way Mercy moved, the tone of his voice, the way he gave orders that showed exactly how he'd be in bed.

"I asked a question, baby." Mercy ran a warm palm down Linc's bare back, cupping his ass cheek. "Expect an answer."

And then he slapped Linc's ass, the sound ringing through the room, the smack of pain causing Linc to hiss out a breath. "Yes."

"You wanted to be bound and helpless on the bed in front of me?"

Another smack, another glorious bite of pain. "Yes," Linc managed, and was rewarded with several more smacks. "Wanted . . . you."

And then fuck, Mercy's tongue was everywhere—trailing down his spine, licking his hole, filling him, sucking him until Linc was writhing—or trying to, since Mercy held firm onto his hips—and begging. Loudly.

That only seemed to fuel Mercy on more. He took his time readying Linc's ass, kept his face buried, teasing with his mouth and his hands, putting fingers inside of him and then playing with his cock, bringing him to the edge and then pulling back.

And all the while, Linc repeated "Mercy" and "yes" and "please" like a chant, a prayer, a promise needing to be kept . . . until finally, he heard the rip of the condom wrapper and then felt Mercy's cock nudge between his cheeks. He used Linc's shoulder for leverage and pushed forward, and Linc's eyes watered, because there was always pain, no matter how well Mercy had played with him. That was part of the game, part of his need . . . part of the fun.

Then Mercy's crown was inside of him and from there, Mercy pressed forward in one long stroke, bottoming out. Linc stilled for a moment, and Mercy did too . . . rubbing Linc's lower back, murmuring, "pretty boy" and "so good" and "so fucking tight," and then Linc was writhing back against him, trying to tug his wrists apart because he needed to hold Mercy. A need so great he didn't understand where it came from.

But somehow, Mercy knew. Pumped in and out of him a few times and then pulled out, undid the cuffs, and turned Linc over before kneeling between his spread legs. And then Mercy was fucking him, nailing his prostate, and Linc? Was wrapped around him, off the bed—so Mercy was supporting all his own weight and Linc's—holding him so goddamned tightly as Mercy blew his mind. Mercy was still mostly clothed, Linc was naked and helpless and coming . . .

Fuck. Linc was breathing hard just thinking about that. A cold shower wasn't going to cut it. He took a long hot one instead, jerked himself twice and yelled in relief and frustration—a mix of curses and Mercy's name.

Mercy heard the yell and his name and raced off the porch and upstairs, only to catch a glimpse of Linc coming behind the partially steamed-up glass shower door.

He watched for a moment, then backed away slowly and quietly headed back downstairs to wait.

It made what he was about to do that much easier.

Everything changed on the sixth day of Mercy's visit, after Linc's fifth night in a row of sneaking out and dancing and drinking his ass off at Bertha's.

He was, as usual, swimming laps in the lake when Mercy showed and watched him doing his laps to burn off the sexual energy that his shower hadn't been able to. But today, Mercy didn't stay by the house, instead walked down to the dock and waited there patiently . . . until Linc got out of the water and shook himself like a dog, silently laughing to himself as he got Mercy wet in the process. And if he and Mercy were talking, if Linc wasn't so fucking angry, he'd laugh and laugh and let Mercy threaten him and then they'd probably fuck, right there on the dock.

But that was the old Linc and Mercy.

"I'm going inside to shower," Linc told him now, but Mercy stood up and blocked his way off the dock with his body.

Linc looked at him and crossed his arms until Mercy finally told him, "I'm here to help you move."

"Move?" he echoed.

"To Havoc."

Linc waited for the punchline, but none came. Not even when he said, "This is a joke, right?"

"Does it look like I'm joking?"

No, Mercy looked serious. Harder than before, and angrier too. "I'm not moving to Havoc."

He tried to walk around Mercy, but Mercy stepped back so he was blocking Linc, yet not touching him. "I'm not asking, I'm telling. Anyone with Havoc ties is being called into the compound. Ask your precious Vann and he'll tell you."

The fact that Mercy might actually be jealous gave Linc the first surge of hope he'd had in months. And obviously, he'd been apprised of Linc's appetite-for-destruction tour. "For how long?"

"As long as it takes. Bram's staying put too. And once this threat is gone, I'll decide where and when you can go."

"You'll decide?" God, he was a fucking parrot.

"You still owe me bond. You've got to work it off . . . by working for me."

Linc couldn't find the words. He could barely meet Mercy's eyes because the pain was too fresh, as if old wounds had reopened, spilling out around them onto the wooden planks of the dock. He shifted and felt a splinter slice into the bottom of his foot, and that pain was a welcome distraction from the emotional one. "What exactly does that entail?"

"Whatever I need it to. And right now? You need to stop fucking around and pack."

"I want to talk to Sweet," Linc demanded.

"He knows. So does Bram," Mercy assured him. "Get packed."

"Get screwed."

"That'll happen—just not in someone else's house."

"Is that what this is all about?"

"Not all—no, it's about protection. And I can't do that effectively unless you're in Havoc."

"But I didn't ask for protection." Linc sighed. "I'm not going."

"You're claimed, Linc."

Linc's eyes narrowed. "Come again?"

"I might not have made this clear before and that's where I fucked up. But make no mistake about it—you're mine, Linc."

Linc's blood surged with heat and hope at those words, but the anger in Mercy's eyes continued to confuse him.

It's not directed at you—it's all inward.

But knowing it and believing it? Two totally different things. "Are you saying this because you think of me as a responsibility?" he asked, and Mercy's nonanswer *was* the answer. Just not the one Linc wanted.

"Besides the fact that you owe the bond, the fact that you fall under my protection is in the Havoc bylaws."

Linc felt a shiver go through him, and Mercy motioned for him to begin walking toward the house. He did so, reluctantly, and told himself it was only because the sun was going down and he was cold.

Mercy continued explaining. "I saved you. We were together. You owe money. By rights, you're mine. This isn't playing MC anymore."

Linc didn't bother saying that he knew that, that he always had, probably more than any of his friends realized. His choices—Mercy's past—had put them on this path, and there was no turning back.

He'd never wanted to anyway.

Vann's words echoed in his mind. *". . . when an MC man saves you . . . you're his. Until he's done with you. And Havoc men? They don't take that lightly. Mercy won't."*

Linc felt like he'd taken a fucking bullet. But there wasn't time to argue. Or really, any way to. As screwed up as it might appear to an outsider, Linc knew he'd bought himself a one-way ticket to MC-ville when he'd gotten involved with Havoc. And it wasn't all fun and games and dancing on the bar at Bertha's. "I'm going to shower and then I'll pack."

If Mercy was surprised at the quick submission, he hid it well.

Mercy wanted to throw the boy down on the bed and fuck him until he became pliant and happy, and if Linc had been in any shape for that, it would've happened.

But he wasn't. And so Mercy had to use his other powers of persuasion—like the fact that Linc still owed money and had an open court case.

Linc had stopped packing and was just standing there.

Mercy prodded him along by saying, "I'll wait and put your bag and hog in the truck."

For a long moment, Mercy thought he wasn't going to move, but finally, and with a clenched jaw, he began to throw clothes and books into a duffel bag . . . muttering the entire time.

This wasn't going to be easy, not with his past coming into his present. It had already fucked him up along with his relationship with

Linc. If he had any hope of repairing it, they'd have to do so where it all began . . . at Havoc.

"How long am I yours for?" Linc asked as he shoved jeans into the bag.

"Until I cut you loose, that's how long."

"Huh. When's that time limit up, Mercy? When you make sure all the Heathens are gone?"

"Did you come to me for bail?"

"Yes."

"Did you come to me to fuck?"

Linc's cheeks flushed. "Yes."

"Then you're mine. More than mine."

"Bounty hunters don't force their charges to live with them."

"They're not Havoc." Linc rolled his eyes like a petulant teenager, and Mercy's palm itched to spank him. "You're lucky I'm mindful of your healing."

"Or what?"

"You'd be bare-assed, over my knee. Keep pushing and it might happen tonight, on my porch."

Linc's cheeks flushed with embarrassment and need, and Mercy was intimately familiar with that look.

"I know you, and I know what you like."

Linc drew his bottom lip into his mouth and shook his head.

"Say what you were going to say."

Linc shook his head. "It was nothing that would help either of us."

Mercy's gut tightened. "But packing and coming to Havoc *will* help you."

Linc turned to face him. "And what's going to help you?"

"The same thing," Mercy said quietly.

You wanted Mercy's attention. How's that working for you now?

And goddammit, Linc wasn't sure how to feel.

Going out, partying, flirting? Hell, that's what made life good and he'd started to feel more like himself. As for work? Well hell, it was something he'd enjoyed before this, but being in Havoc and keeping secrets was TNT primed to explode.

He could talk to Bram about it . . . but Bram would freak. He was still coming down off his own mission from hell involving the Heathens, and they didn't need more shitty shit to bond over.

Besides, telling Bram was like telling Sweet, which was as good as telling Mercy. Same with telling Rush, because that would run right to Ryker and again, to Mercy. All roads led to Mercy.

Beyond that, Castle mandated secrecy. So yeah, none of this was going to work. Getting out now, until things calmed down and maybe forever, was the best bet all around. It wasn't like he didn't have other shit to figure out beyond work, anyway.

Fuck. He shook all of that off and continued packing. He didn't want to leave, because of the lake and the peace, but shit was getting heavier and having men guard him an hour outside of Havoc was pulling resources.

Linc had friends inside of Havoc. He cared about what happened to the club, but he didn't want to be tied down to club rules himself.

Too late. He'd known what he was getting into. Do the crime, do the time and all that good shit.

"Need help?" Mercy was at his bedroom door, leaning there lazily and looking too fucking good. Angry and moody and biker-ish.

Fuckable.

Linc sighed. "I can carry shit."

"Yeah? So can I." Mercy brushed past him, shouldered his bags, and walked out, whistling for Linc to follow him.

"Like I'm a fucking dog," Linc muttered.

"I could put a collar on you." Mercy had turned fast so Linc bumped into him. Now, Mercy was tracing his collarbone. "Is that what you want—to show everyone you know you're owned?"

Linc growled, but he couldn't deny how good that touch felt. As soon as Mercy's hand moved, he felt cold and he shivered.

Mercy frowned in concern. "You getting sick?" He put his hand on Linc's forehead. Without thinking, Linc sank against it. "You feel okay."

So does this.

Mercy stayed there for a second as if considering. "There's one more thing we need to get clear on."

Linc sighed. "Only one more?"

"That man who visits you here? He's not allowed on Havoc property."

"He's just a friend. This is his place," Linc said.

Mercy raised his brows. "He gave you a house? You must've been a good lay for him."

Mercy's goad hit the mark, because Linc's eyes went cold as ice when he answered. "Yeah, I was. He loved every fucking second of it. But you have firsthand experience in how good of a lay I am, right, Mercy?"

"You need to back off."

"Don't want to hear about how I went down on my knees for him?" Mercy pushed him against the wall, but Linc let him, didn't fight back. Not physically at least, but fire snapped in his eyes. "Want to hear about how he filled my ass when I needed it? How he held me after I came?"

Mercy's mouth came down on his—to shut him up. To erase that man—and any other—from Linc's mouth, his thoughts, to imprint him and only him on the younger man, so the only name—and cock—Linc remembered was his.

His tongue fought with Linc's, and Linc's hands stayed down by his sides and not on Mercy . . . but after several moments of Mercy grinding against him, Linc was arching into him, banging his fists against the wall in frustration.

Finally, he gave up and wrapped his arms around Mercy and tried to climb him like a tree.

But Mercy felt Linc's wince, a reminder that the man he held had been hurt—very—and he wasn't ready for any kind of sex, rough or otherwise.

Mercy lowered him gently, because Linc looked pale. His hand went to Linc's side and rubbed.

"C'mon, Linc. Let's get you . . ."

"To bed?" Linc snorted. "I'm fine. You're only worried because of Castle. Otherwise you wouldn't even be here. Don't want me, don't want anyone else to have me."

"Is that what Castle wants? To have you?" Mercy asked quietly.

"I don't think he'd say no if I asked."

Mercy knew Linc would try to push every single button he had—knew it and prepared for it, and Linc was still winning this round. "What about you, Linc? Would you say no? Put a stop to it? Or would you do it and think about me the entire time?"

"Fuck you, Mercy."

"Yeah, that's what I thought."

CHAPTER 9

AND WE WERE GLOWIN' LIKE THE METAL ON THE EDGE OF A KNIFE

"Wait, what?" Bram asked. "What the ever-loving fuck is this?"

Sweet watched him, tamping his patience down for the man he loved after delivering the news about Linc's coming to Havoc. "Bram, Linc's coming here, where he'll be protected. Focus on that."

Bram stared at him, the damned defiance still completely seductive. "Linc didn't want to come here—he's happy at the lake house."

"You're the one who worries about him constantly when he's there without you," Sweet reminded him.

"I'll worry about him wherever he is for the rest of his life," Bram shot back.

"It's within Mercy's right to make the decision to bring him here."

"With your approval?"

"Mercy saved him. And he saved you," Sweet pointed out, sidestepping the question a bit and trying to avoid bloodshed. Bram had been equally claimed—he just didn't want to think about it now. Sweet would remind him.

"And Mercy got Linc into this," Bram countered. He shook his head and clenched his jaw until he finally managed, "I'll focus on the fact that Linc is safe."

"And he'll be with you." Sweet put his arms around Bram. "It's going to be okay."

"Because you will it to be so, right?"

Sweet let a slow smile slide across his face. "Yeah, baby."

And finally, Bram smiled back, looking less worried. "After you finish fucking me, we're going to talk more about this."

"I'm not going to be finished for a long time," Sweet assured him.

Rush and Ryker were playing *Grand Theft Auto* on Ryker's massive flat-screen when Ryker delivered the news to him casually.

"Hey, Mercy's bringing Linc back."

Rush frowned and dug in harder, assuming Ryker was trying to distract him from the game he was winning. "As in, they're getting back together?"

"As in, dragging him back, caveman-style, into Havoc for protection."

It was enough for Rush to put down the controller and forfeit the damned game. "Ryk, that doesn't work for me. At all."

Ryker frowned. "Seriously?"

"Seriously." Rush realized he was actually furious and in serious need of calming down. The problem with that was that Ryker loved a challenge.

"Take off your clothes."

Rush jumped up. "Holy shit—talk about cavemen. I mean, how the fuck is it possible for Mercy to ignore Linc for months—"

"Slept outside his door for months—Linc's the one who banned him," Ryker reasoned.

"And now suddenly Mercy gets to act like he owns Linc—"

"Linc's been going out, doing things he shouldn't, and Mercy does own him," Ryker continued.

"And how the fuck are you all *okay* with it?"

"And now I'm asking you to take off your clothes," Ryker repeated. "If you make me ask a third time"—which he knew Rush would—"I'll be happy and you will be too, just not at first."

Rush crossed his arms.

"Fair enough," Ryker murmured and stood.

Rush put his arms up. "I realize permission is an old-fashioned concept but . . ."

Ryker sighed. "Linc's been claimed."

"'Claimed'?" Rush repeated doubtfully.

"Yeah. So are you."

"You're . . . joking? Right?"

"You sayin' the idea of being claimed doesn't make your dick hard?" Ryker asked, his smile knowing, and yeah, Rush's dick suddenly equaled hard. "Because you didn't seem to mind it when I chased your ass all over God's green earth."

Rush backed up but Ryker was stalking toward him as he spoke, with a look in his eyes Rush was intimately familiar with. "Ryk, we're not talking about—"

"I was." Ryker made contact, tugged him close. "Do you trust me?"

"With my life," Rush said, without a second's hesitation. "With my goddamned heart and soul."

"And here I thought I was the romantic. Now, take off your clothes and let's get to the *showing how I claimed you* part."

Rush considered his options, and since Ryker was both leading him and stripping him at the same time, he saw no reason to not let Ryker re-explain this whole claiming thing, for clarification purposes.

Because you could never have too much knowledge.

Two hours later, Linc stood on the porch of Mercy's house, nestled in the protection of the Havoc compound, and it was all so damned familiar and yet it felt like he was moving in with a total stranger.

Mercy walked back and forth, brushing by him several times as he brought Linc's belongings inside. When he was done, instead of demanding Linc come inside, which is what Linc had expected to happen, he just left the door open and didn't come back out.

Because you're safe here.

Linc wanted to laugh at that. Being with Mercy was the most dangerous thing for him at the moment.

But after several moments, he followed Mercy's path inside the house and found him in the kitchen, sitting at the table, nursing a beer. "Your stuff's in the bedroom."

Linc had expected him to say *guest bedroom* but he didn't question it, just walked upstairs to Mercy's room and, sure enough, his stuff was there.

"Fuck," he muttered.

Mercy came in behind him and if he heard that, he ignored it. "I made room for your stuff in the closets and drawers and bookshelves. You're not living out of bags and boxes, got it?"

"Yes, sir," Linc said, without a trace of irony.

Mercy nodded. "I've got church tonight. You can't leave the compound without my okay."

"Don't you mean your permission?" And there was his old friend, sarcasm.

But Mercy seemed . . . almost amused. "If you want to call it that, feel free to. Again, no leaving without my okay and at least two Havoc members with you at all times. And Rush? He doesn't count."

"Now you're in charge of him too?"

Mercy just gave him a small, know-it-all smile.

"I know what you do now. You're an enforcer."

"Does that bother you?"

"Does it bother you?"

"It's what I was born to do," Mercy told him. "For Havoc. I never wanted to do it for Heathens. Now come on—I made dinner."

Linc was surprised Mercy had admitted that much. He followed Mercy into the kitchen and sat at the table. Mercy put a big bowl of pasta in front of him and Linc realized how hungry he actually was. He took a bite of the pasta and fuck, it was good. He'd almost forgotten what a good cook Mercy was. It reminded Linc of all the late-night meals they'd shared before . . .

He shook his head so he didn't have to complete that memory, put the fork down. "Why now?"

"Because everyone knows who I am. Even the Heathens who are left know. And I owe it to Havoc—and to you—to stop hiding."

"So I'm an obligation."

"I don't mean it like that. Not the way you're thinking."

"Okay, sure. So am I supposed to just stay in the house and wait to feel better?"

"No, you're going to work."

"Right. Because I owe you money."

"The last time you came, Linc? Who were you thinking about?" Mercy asked, and Linc's cheeks flushed, even as he looked away. "That's what I thought."

"Don't get cocky, Mercy. I didn't give you an answer."

"Yeah, you did, baby. Because I heard you before. That was my goddamn name you called out when you came all over the tiles."

"Fuck." Linc shook his head.

"Tell me what you were imagining me doing to you."

"No." Linc's voice was a rough whisper.

"Was I sucking you off? Fucking you? Were you over my lap?"

Linc made a strangled sound in his throat. "Why? Because it makes you hard thinking about it? Do you think about me when you're jacking off, Mercy?"

"Every goddamned time," Mercy promised.

Linc moved toward Mercy, suddenly fucking furious—with Mercy, with himself, with everything. He yanked Mercy toward him and kissed him, an angry, unforgiving kiss . . . and Mercy matched his anger and gave it right back to him in spades. Mercy held Linc in place, his hands twisting in Linc's hair, and Linc had never felt so unbroken in his life.

He pulled away first, knowing he couldn't take this further right now. And even though he was breathing fast, cheeks hot, staring up at Mercy, he was pleased with his version of getting in the last word.

Mercy left, warning that he wouldn't be gone long. Linc paced around the house, thought about taking his stuff out of the drawers and putting it back into his bag just to piss Mercy off and ultimately decided against it. Not enough bang for his buck.

So he called Rush, who groaned. "You're not asking me to sneak you out of here already, are you?"

"What kind of friend would I be if I didn't?" Linc demanded.

"Jesus Christ, Ryker's going to kill me."

"Just don't wear anything of his so he can't track you," Linc instructed. "Pull behind the garage here so I can get into the trunk."

"The trunk? You're not allowed off Havoc at all?"

"Nope," Linc said happily. "And it's a stupid rule, made to be broken."

"We've already broken so many rules. How is it still so much fun?"

"Because it always is."

"Fine," Rush bit out. "But they're on their way home from church—Ryker just texted me."

"Tomorrow night, then."

"The trunk's never going to work."

"The woods, then—north side of the compound. It's the least populated area and there's only a natural barrier. You can leave and pull along the road and I'll come through the woods."

Rush breathed out a sigh. "This is ridiculous. Maybe if you just asked Mercy—"

"Like you used to ask Ryker?" Linc shot back.

"Fucker. Tomorrow night," Rush promised before hanging up. And that was a good thing because several minutes later, Mercy's footsteps were headed up the stairs. Linc was half under the covers, staring out the window, his back to Mercy. He heard the slide of Mercy's clothing hit the ground and felt the bed dip next to him.

He waited, tense, to see if any part of Mercy would touch him . . . and he wasn't sure if he was more relieved that it didn't happen . . . or more angry.

There would be no sneaking out that night—not with Mercy lying next to him in the dark.

Lying there, not touching him. Fuck, this was too hard. Harder than he'd thought. There was also the fear of having a nightmare. He needed a better plan than never sleeping again.

He shifted and yanked the covers higher over him.

Mercy sighed. "Why don't you just get some sleep?"

"How do you know I'm not?" Linc demanded.

"Because you're making me seasick."

The times they'd spent together in bed hadn't involved much sleeping on either of their parts. What would happen if he jerked himself off? Would Mercy know? Stop him . . . join him?

You're not ready. For any of this.

Next to him, Mercy sighed again. "Touch your cock, Linc."

Linc's breath caught. He blinked hard and stared into the dark.

"Are you going to ignore what I'm telling you? Was a time I'd tell you to touch your cock that you listened. Unless you suddenly don't want pleasure anymore."

Linc blinked back tears of relief and let his hand slide down his abdomen and into his sweats. He wasn't wearing underwear, so it was easy to free his cock and then palm it. "Okay," he whispered.

"Stroke yourself—slowly," Mercy told him. "Touch your balls with your free hand. Roll them."

Linc did what Mercy asked without thinking.

"Use a finger—press it against your slit," Mercy instructed. Linc did so and hissed out a breath at his own intrusion. "You're wet, right, baby?"

"Yes," Linc managed.

"Taste yourself." Linc brought his finger to his mouth, the salty flavor strong on his tongue. "Keep stroking—faster now. I'm not giving you long to come. If you miss out, you'll sleep with that hard-on all night."

Fuck. Linc began to stroke in earnest, wondering if Mercy would really punish him.

He closed his eyes and realized it was too dark and they flew open. He stopped stroking.

As if Mercy knew, he said, "Baby, keep going. Pretend we're in the alley behind Bertha's. I've got you pressed against the wall, and I'm holding your cock . . . and we're not alone out there."

Linc could picture that—although most people in the alleyway were otherwise occupied, there was definitely voyeurism happening.

"Are you with me, Linc?"

"Yes."

"Tell me what's happening."

Linc stroked his hard cock faster, his words blurring together. "You're not blocking me with your body . . . you're standing to the side so anyone can watch. And you're going to make me come."

"Your cock's dripping now. And you're loving that people are watching. You don't know if I'm going to turn you over and fuck you when you're done, or if I'm going to call someone over to do the job."

"Fuck." Linc's hips surged off the bed as if Mercy's words were touching him. His balls tightened and ropes of come shot across his belly and chest as he moaned softly.

"Good boy, Linc," Mercy told him softly.

In his postorgasmic haze, Linc felt the bed shift as Mercy got up. And then Linc felt his belly and chest and hand and cock being cleaned by a warm, wet cloth rasping over his skin. Mercy's touch.

Linc's eyes met his in the dark and, for the first time in as long as he could remember, he smiled at Mercy.

CHAPTER 10

HOPE IT GIVES YOU HELL

Linc walked warily into the bail bonds shop. It was just before nine in the morning, and Mercy flipped the sign and didn't relock the door behind them.

"You're carrying?" he asked Linc, who nodded. "Good. So am I. So's Tug." He pointed across the street to where Tug sat, outside the restaurant at one of the tables, and Tug waved back.

"Great. Where's my brother? In sniper position on the roof?" Linc muttered, and when Mercy barely glanced at him, Linc was out the door, looking up at the roof. "You've got to be fucking kidding me."

Mercy was dragging him back inside. "Don't give away his position. And it's not Bram—it's Shaman, okay?"

"I don't know Shaman, so no, it's not okay. None of this is. Fuck." Linc shoved Mercy away from him. "If I need this much protection to work here, I might as well have just stayed back at Havoc. Or at the damned lake."

"Where you'd just go stir-crazy and eventually do something stupid," Mercy countered. "Like tequila."

"Tequila is never stupid," Linc deadpanned.

"You think we don't know what you and Rush were planning? Sneaking through the woods and getting into the trunk of Rush's car once you hit the road?"

Linc stood stock-still. It'd been a good plan, dammit, and now it was all wasted. Havoc would probably put up a fortified wall in that spot. "Now you're spying on me? And with Rush's help?"

Mercy swore. "Rush knew nothing about it."

"Bullshit." And now Linc had no one to trust, not in the sense that all his private thoughts wouldn't be blasted throughout Havoc. "I know I'm weak. I don't need to be made to feel weaker, okay?"

"You think this is about you being weak?"

"That's exactly what this is about." Linc stuffed his hands into his pockets. "You know what? Just show me what to do."

Mercy looked suspicious at his sudden compliance, but he also looked guilty as fuck, which was what Linc counted on. "You've been in here before, albeit on the other side of the counter. But you know the drill. We either get a call or a walk-in. Someone's in jail and needs bail money. We have them fill out the forms, do a background and bank check to make sure they're good for what they say they're good for. And then we post the bond."

"Got it."

"Really? You're that quick of a study?"

"It's not rocket science." Linc paused, then asked hopefully. "What happens if they skip?"

"Then *I* go look for them."

"Right. So *I'm* just sitting here, doing the paperwork." Linc shook his head and wondered if it would take days or hours for him to go crazy.

Hours. Definitely hours, Linc decided after filing his twentieth bond form. He rubbed his temples. His body ached from sitting in one place for so long, because he didn't even have to get up to file.

Mercy was at his goddamned elbow on the phone. Across the street, Tug was also on the phone and who the hell knew what Shaman was doing? But Linc? He knew what *he* was going to do.

He mouthed, *Bathroom*, to Mercy, who waved him off . . . and then Linc went down the hall, closed the bathroom door but remained outside of it, disabled the alarm on the back door in three seconds flat and went outside. In the lot behind the shop sat several cars, one of which was Tug's. Linc hot-wired it and went out the other entrance to the lot, and wondered why they didn't have anyone at the back of the lot.

Too late, he realized they had . . . and that person was in the back seat of the car he was driving. "I'm not stopping," he said now. "And fuck you."

"Hey, this wasn't my idea. Trust me." Rush sighed.

"You sold me out."

"You think I knew they were listening to us? My fucking ass is sore as hell from the chewing out I got from Ryker."

Linc snorted. "Are you turning me in? Because otherwise, it's going to get even sorer."

Rush hopped over into the front seat. "Take a right up ahead."

Rush steered him into the Hangmen's clubhouse, where Noah was waiting. With Tequila. Linc was never more grateful for the promise of bad decisions sure to follow.

"About fucking time they let you out," he said as he hugged Linc.

"'Let me out' isn't exactly what happened," Linc told him.

"Don't tell me anything they can torture out of me," Noah said. He was dating Casey's daughter, and Casey was the president of Hangmen. Noah wasn't prospecting, but he was working with the Hangmen, and with Jethro. "Come on—I'm working on something you'll appreciate."

They followed Noah into the back of the garage, where he'd carved out a space to work on his own designs, which included restoring a cherry-red, vintage 1979 Porsche 911.

"She's gorgeous," Rush murmured, running a hand over the hood, and Linc smiled at the look on his friend's face. He'd never met anyone who'd been so into cars as Rush was. "Exploding clutch?"

"Been driving me crazy," Noah told him and soon, he and Rush were under the hood, talking grease monkey, and Linc hoisted himself up on the workbench to oversee the process, beer in hand, radio blasting . . . and he could almost pretend that everything was just fine. At least for a while.

When Casey came in, Linc wondered if this was the end of his merry excursion, if the Hangmen's president had been called to send him and Rush back on home, complete with escorts. But Casey said hi to Rush and ambled easily over to where Linc sat, grabbing himself a beer before settling in on the high bench next to him.

"How's it going, Linc?" Casey's voice was deep. Smoky. He was a sexy fucker, all ginger-haired, strong-jawed, goatee-wearing. He was also heavily tattooed, tall and lanky, but still well-built; he was bisexual, never married, and he'd raised his daughter as a single dad.

"It's going," was all Linc could manage.

Casey had hit on Rush—and helped him through a difficult time when things weren't going well with Ryker—but he'd never screwed with their relationship once it had been established.

Now, Casey snorted at his answer. "Heard you've been claimed."

"Is there anyone in the free world who hasn't?" Linc couldn't keep the edge of pissed-off-edness out of his voice. "Like I'm wearing a goddamned brand."

When he glanced over at Casey, he saw understanding in the man's expression. "You really don't want that brand?"

Linc shifted. "I'd like a fucking choice." Christ, was there truth serum in this goddamned beer? "Forget it. I figure you'll report this back to him."

"Got a smart mouth. I like it," Casey told him. Linc settled his gaze on the man's dark-green eyes. "Need a new place to stay, babe? Got plenty of room here."

As much as he liked the idea, Linc knew that would cost him. "That's kind of like going from the frying pan into the fire, right?"

Casey grinned. "Slow burn can be fun with the right person."

"I can't deny that." Linc accepted another beer from him.

"Offer stands for as long as it's needed," Casey said, before moving their conversation onto cars and Harleys and the like, spinning easily, and Linc didn't feel uncomfortable.

After half an hour, Rush and Noah emerged from under the hood, Casey went to do whatever it was Casey did when he wasn't flirting and running things, and Linc had another beer and a couple of shots and felt his energy kick up several notches.

Together, he and his friends could do a lot of damage—which to them usually started out with the words, *We should go out tonight*.

"We should go out tonight," Linc told them now.

"Why do you do this to yourself?" Rush asked and Noah snorted.

Linc shrugged. "Because I'm complicated."

"I'm complicated. Layered, even," Rush argued.

"You just want to steal cars and get laid."

Rush considered that. "I can't argue with that assessment."

"I know."

"Did you ever stop to think that you purposely complicate? So you don't need to get close?"

"Okay, Freud, I've had enough." He glanced at Noah. "You in?"

"Of course. I'll even drive. Where're we headed?"

"Bertha's," Linc said firmly. "They'll catch up with us eventually. Might as well have some fun."

"Yeah, they're here, just like you said," Tug told Mercy now. "I'm waiting outside."

"I figured Linc would have more fun if he thought there was some evade and escape happening," Mercy told him from where he still sat in the bonds shop.

"Did you figure on them continuing their E&E party by easing on down the road to Bertha's?" Tug asked.

And no, he hadn't counted on Linc going to Bertha's afterward, but Linc, being Linc, had to push it to whatever limit there was . . . and then inch it just over that final line of limits. Because he could.

"In other news, I didn't see any Heathens—or their spies—anywhere near the shop," Tug continued. "Shaman didn't either."

"They're regrouping—don't let their quiet fool you," Mercy told them seriously.

"Trust me—we're not letting our guard down. Not for a second," Tug assured him. "But Mercy . . . eventually . . ."

"Linc's going to need to get back to doing Linc things without all the backup. I know." Mercy shook his head. "He's not ready yet. He thinks he is. But . . ."

"But you'll know exactly when that is?" Tug asked hesitatingly. "This is going to result in war between you two. You know that, right?"

"I'm counting on it."

CHAPTER 11

TELL ME BABY, DON'T THEY MAKE A MEDICINE FOR HEARTBREAK

When Linc, Rush, and Noah arrived at Bertha's, the crowd was already in full swing. There was a DJ tonight and the dance floor was full.

Noah grabbed another bottle of tequila from the bar and brought it over to the table where Vann was already planted. Linc didn't bother to ask if he'd known about the escape, because the answer was undoubtedly yes.

After several more shots and a couple of beers, Linc was feeling the happy buzz . . . and the hollowed-out feeling again. To combat it, he hit the dance floor, with Rush and Noah and was quickly joined by Vann.

And Tug and Boomer.

And Shaman, who turned out to be a cool guy and promised to teach him about the newest in sniper rifles.

And then Jethro and Casey showed up and they danced too. Casey gave him a big hug, lifting him off his feet, but gently enough Linc didn't feel it in his ribs.

Sweet wasn't there this time, which meant Bram wasn't either.

Of course, as usual, there was no sign of Mercy.

Bathroom, Linc mouthed to Rush and threaded his way through the crowds on the dance floor, feeling Vann at his back. He was grateful, not angry, because if he thought about the way the bodies pressed his for too long, he'd panic.

Finally, he found a pocket of space in the hallway by the bathrooms. There was a small line that moved quickly and Vann had left him alone at some point. Linc pissed, washed up, and headed out . . . and was stopped by a handsome guy, probably around his age. Maybe he'd even been military.

"Hey, you're Linc, right?" the guy said. "I'm Louie."

"Hey," Linc said.

"You hang out with Mercy sometimes, right?"

"Yeah, sometimes."

"I haven't seen him in a couple of weeks. Can you pass him my number?"

Linc frowned. "For what?"

"C'mon, man—the same reason you were making out with him in the bar. He's a good fuck. He likes to spread it around—he's fucking insatiable. Am I right?"

Linc felt numb at the truth of what Louie was saying. When he and Mercy started fucking, Mercy had been all over him, and to be fair, Linc had been the same. But three times a day was normal for them and Linc had a feeling it wouldn't have waned if things had gone along as they'd been.

But they didn't.

"He use his cuffs on you?" Louie continued. "We were here, so that didn't happen but one of my buddies got the full treatment."

Instead of answering—because the answer would've been a resounding yes—Linc took the paper with the name and number on it. "I'll pass the message along."

"Cool, thanks. It's not like these guys settle down—that's what makes it so good, right?" Louie winked.

Rush was suddenly behind him, a hand on his back, and Linc figured he'd heard enough. The hand was part support and no doubt to stop him if he lunged for Louie. But Linc felt no such impulse.

"So Mercy was fucking you?" Rush asked.

"Yeah. A lot."

"And you felt it was important to tell him this why?" Rush demanded.

"Why not? I wasn't the only one here that he was fucking. Ask around—you'll get all the truth you want. Besides, there's enough Mercy to go around." Louie smiled and headed off into the crowd.

"Maybe he was just making it up. Wishful thinking," Rush offered.

"He wasn't making it up," Linc said dully. Because he knew firsthand just how insatiable Mercy was—and how much he liked being in control. Because the only way they'd know that for sure is if they'd been with him.

It gave Linc a small measure of comfort to know that he'd been able to keep up with Mercy—barely—and that they'd spent so much time together that Mercy hadn't had time for extracurricular activity.

Louie had meant no harm, had no idea of the devastation that had begun the slow climb through Linc's body and into his goddamned soul.

But this was not the time or place to break apart. "I need more tequila."

"Good. Because the karaoke's just about to start."

After another round of singing—during which he discovered that Casey sounded a lot like Barry White—Linc headed out the back door to the small alleyway along the side of the club. It was protected on both ends by bouncers, fenced in, and there were several couples out here already, in various stages of making out.

He leaned against the brick wall, letting the air cool him. It wouldn't sober him—he wouldn't let it. Sober wasn't something he wanted right now.

The door opened and he felt someone approach. He assumed it would be Vann, but it wasn't. It was Jethro, holding a wet towel.

He offered it wordlessly, and when Linc nodded, he carefully wiped Linc's face down. It felt so damned good—both the cool and the actual touch.

Especially the touch. Linc closed his eyes and imagined it was Mercy. When he opened them, Jethro seemed like he knew what Linc was doing, but he didn't seem upset about it. "How're you doing, kid?"

"'Kid'? Seriously with that shit," Linc muttered and Jethro smiled warmly at him. "I'm better. Much."

"Yeah, heard that before." Jethro leaned against the wall, and Linc turned his head. "Heard you're out of Castle's place."

"Yep."

"Back on the job already?"

"Fuck no."

"Good. Too soon."

"To go back or to make decisions about going back?"

"Both," Jethro affirmed.

Castle and Jethro went way back, just slightly longer than Linc and Castle did, and so Linc was one of the few outside of the MCs who knew who—*what*—Jethro was . . . which was undercover ATF and also a member of the Hangmen MC, formerly the Watchers MC, which had been Jethro's father's MC.

The president of the Hangmen knew—Casey was a cool motherfucker who appreciated the inside knowledge without the law coming down on him. Jethro's job was to take out MCs like Heathens and Project X, and so there was a lot of trust in him after three years.

Jethro was a full member of the Hangmen—there were some things he didn't participate in because of his job, but he'd told Linc that he loved being a part of something bigger, of that kind of brotherhood, and if it came between the MC and the ATF, he'd choose the MC, hands-down.

"You're not okay, are you?" Jethro ran a knuckle under Linc's chin, forcing him to meet his eyes.

"Not even close, but I'm trying."

"Shouldn't have to try. Shouldn't be here alone."

"I'm not alone."

"If you're not with the man who claimed you, you're alone." Jethro shook his head, and the knuckle moved, tracing its way down Linc's neck, and then it became a fingertip, playing along Linc's collarbone.

It had been safe to flirt with Vann, and for Vann to flirt back . . . especially because right now, Mercy wasn't all that safe for Linc and vice versa.

But Jethro was the furthest thing from safe. Linc's belly clenched, but it wasn't in a bad way, like it had earlier. No, it was in that nice way, when flirting threatened to go a step further and suddenly? Linc was more than okay with that.

And Jethro? He could push Linc harder than Vann could, because he wasn't Havoc, and even though the clubs were friends, he didn't have to follow their rules. That had been evidenced when Rush was running from Ryker and Casey tried his hardest to get into Rush's pants.

Linc cleared his throat. "You're just doing it to piss Mercy off."

Jethro shook his head slowly. "That's what *you're* doing. I don't give a fuck about Mercy. He's not my club. Not your club either. The only reason I'm holding back? Is you."

Jethro's eyes swept over him . . . and he didn't look at Linc like he was broken.

"Can you just kiss me?" Linc asked.

"Comparison shopping?"

"Maybe."

"I can tell you the outcome already, if it helps." Jethro kissed him, a slow, heated, gorgeous fucking kiss that made Linc's entire body heat . . . but it didn't erase his longing for Mercy.

If anything, it made it worse.

Jethro brushed hair out of Linc's eyes. "I figured."

"Sorry."

"Don't be. I'm not. I'm available to do it again and again, just to make sure. Maybe, one of these days, I won't know the outcome." He jerked his head toward the door. "We need to go back in."

"I'll go first."

Jethro watched Linc disappear inside, with one lingering look over his shoulder. Jethro remained against the wall, but turned his head to stare across the alley. "It's not like that, Vann."

"The only reason I haven't shot out both your knees is because I know that."

"Yeah, you and what army?"

Vann came forward and walked up to him. Jethro's back was already to the wall and Vann pressed him there. "I don't need an army, Jethro. Want me to show you?"

Jethro stared into Vann's dark eyes. "Are you pissed that I didn't kiss you?"

"You serious, bro? Because I got no interest in that."

"In kissing? Or kissing me?"

"I don't think you need to worry about who I kiss."

"Who do you kiss?" Jethro asked.

"Why the third degree? You're the one kissing someone else's man."

Jethro shook his head slowly, staring at Vann. "Does he seem like someone else's man to you?"

"They're going through shit. Your interfering isn't cool."

Jethro cocked a brow. "I'm not here to do what's *cool*. I'm not Havoc."

"But you want to fuck Havoc."

"Right now? Yes." Jethro let his gaze run up and down Vann's body.

"Right now I want to punch you."

"Fuck or fight? Same thing." Jethro smiled and slid away toward the parking lot. Vann forced himself not to look over his shoulder when he walked back into Bertha's.

Linc sat at the table, nursing a beer and watching Rush dancing with a group of Havoc old ladies.

Vann sat next to him and threw an arm around the back of Linc's chair. "You fucked since what happened to you, babe?"

Linc snorted, because that question? Hadn't been expected. "Are you a sex therapist in your spare time?"

"I could be." Vann raised a brow. "I take it that's a no."

Linc did his shot and Vann's, then chased them with nearly an entire beer.

"That's a no, but you want to," Vann amended with a smile. Linc was grateful he hadn't brought up the Jethro kiss, even though he was completely sure that's what sparked this conversation. "Hear you're at Havoc now."

"Yeah, good news about being *claimed* travels fast," Linc snarked. Vann put a palm around the back of his neck and it immediately centered him. How Vann knew he needed it was a whole other story.

"I told you, it's his right."

"What about mine?" He met Vann's eyes.

"I think that when someone's not ready to make his own decisions, sometimes he's got to let someone else do it for him."

Linc sighed. "It's not like I have a choice."

"That's the point." Vann took up his own beer. "You can't fuck around with an MC like Havoc and treat the men like toys."

"I didn't— I wasn't . . ." Linc sputtered.

Vann sighed. "You're lookin' for attention . . . and you got it."

Fuck, he was in trouble. "Mercy was fucking around on me when I was being held captive," he blurted out.

If Vann was surprised, he didn't let on. "The man thought you left him."

Great, so Vann was going to defend him. "Yes, him and everyone else."

Vann starred at him. "Did Mercy claim you before you left?"

"He never said the words."

"But everyone knew you were with him?"

"Yes, I guess. I thought it was about the bond."

Vann considered that. "Who told you about Mercy fucking around?"

"Not Mercy." He leaned back. "He's with me out of obligation. That's not helping me."

"I understand you—way more than you know," Vann told him. "You decided to go out because Mercy said that you couldn't."

Linc couldn't argue with that, so he let it go. "What's really going on with Havoc? Is everyone really on high alert?"

Vann looked troubled, took his arm off the back of Linc's chair and leaned in close, his voice low. "Kill Devils are headed this way. They're promising to patch in Heathens who swear their loyalty. And they're bringing a white supremacist drug trade—meth and ecstasy—with them."

Linc took a breath, trying to stave off the panic he felt every time he heard the name Heathens. "It's like the war—it never ends. New soldiers come in. It's like sticking your hand in a bucket of water. You take it out, the water fills right back in."

Vann, who Linc suspected had been to war himself, maybe in more ways than one, nodded. "Mercy's taking a more active role. His choice," he added quickly. "I'm sure he'd tell you if . . ."

"*If* I let him talk to me?" Linc shrugged. "How'd you get so wise?"

Vann smiled, with no light behind it. "I lost someone."

"And there's no one else who can fill the holes?"

"Guess we both know it's not easy."

It was Linc's turn to throw an arm around the back of Vann's chair protectively. "How about we take each other's advice from here on out?"

"You gonna play matchmaker, little boy?"

Linc took no offense to the *little boy* part. "I think I might."

CHAPTER 12

PRIVATE FEARS IN PUBLIC PLACES

Sweet was in the clubhouse with Mercy when he got a call from Vann. As Mercy watched, he figured it wasn't good news and assumed it had to do with Linc. And tequila.

"What's up?" Mercy asked. "Vann bringing him home?"

"Rush is, eventually," Sweet started. "Listen, if Linc was mine . . ."

Fuck. "Something to say to me?"

"More than you want to hear." Sweet took a swig from his beer. "Linc's trying to move on. He wants to do it with you, but if you don't give him what he needs, he's going other places."

"Is Vann one of those other places?"

"He's Havoc. He wouldn't do that. But Jethro's another story."

Mercy stared at him. "Jethro hit on him?"

"Yeah, he did. He doesn't have to follow our rules. He kissed Linc because you wouldn't."

Mercy swallowed his anger—and it was a hard goddamned swallow. "He's not ready."

"You know his body better than he does?"

"If things happen too soon, he'll—"

"Freak? Rather have him freak with you right? Unless you're done with him in that way. If yes, cut him loose. Because honestly, he's acting like you already have. And obviously, people are making moves."

Fuck. He hadn't heeded Vann's warning from yesterday and now this? Linc having fun, yes, that was cool . . . and what Mercy had wanted for him. "All I can do is watch him and protect him, whether he wants it or not—and be there when he finally breaks through."

"So that includes letting other guys kiss him? Because I'm sure Jethro will be thrilled to keep pressing the issue, and next time, it might not stop at a kiss. And then what?"

Mercy's face hardened. "I betrayed Linc too. I fucked around while he was gone."

"So tit for tat?"

"I won't be his obligation," Mercy said finally. His past fucked with him daily. And Linc only knew a portion of it—maybe the most horrible part of his history . . . the culmination of years of systematic abuse by the Heathens. "He blames me, Sweet . . . and he should."

"Did you ever tell him that being with a Havoc man could bring him trouble? That he needed to stick close to Havoc in general?"

"I knew he was a free bird, that he couldn't settle down." And any time Linc had spent with him had been a beautiful goddamned thing. He treasured every memory.

"Mercy, quit the guilt shit and take what you want. If that's him, take him before it's too late," Sweet warned as he slid off the stool.

Mercy stayed in the clubhouse for several more minutes . . . then he got up and punched the wall with the side of his fist—which still left a nice sized dent in the plaster—and he walked out of the clubhouse and got on his bike.

He rode patrols most of the night, then once he'd settled down, went to go make sure Linc knew who he belonged to.

But Linc wasn't ready yet, as much as he wanted to be—as much as Mercy wanted him to be—and pushing him in that direction would be a mistake.

He'd learned that a while ago. After helping Misha out of a similar situation. She'd made him understand that, just because her body felt ready, it didn't mean her mind was. It was all wrong.

No, Mercy needed to let Linc get back to being Linc, no matter how hard it was for Mercy to watch it happen, watch Linc flirt with danger, and Mercy needed to let him. Had to trust that the bond between them would strengthen as it healed.

But just because he had to wait didn't mean he was going to take chances. No, he was about to put safeguards in place.

First, he called Jethro. "Touch him again and you're dead."

Jethro laughed. "I don't answer to you, fucker. But you're the one not giving him what he needs. Don't be surprised when other men offer."

"I know exactly what he needs."

"Yeah, he needs you, Mercy. So whatever you're doing? Try not to fuck it up." Jethro hung up, and Mercy decided he was going to beat the shit out of Jethro the next time he saw him.

"Got the 411 on Havoc from Vann," Linc said as Rush pushed his car past a death-defying speed on the run back toward Havoc. Vann and Tug were following, along with some other Havoc members charged with getting them home safely. Rush took that as a challenge to lose all of them and the merry race became a roller coaster on the highway home.

"Ryker already told me before I left that the Kill Devils are coming to take over Heathens. Trying to patch them in. Take over the drug trade and make it bigger and better."

Linc nodded, then put his head back and closed his eyes. To him, Rush's driving was sure and fast. Soothing even.

Rush sighed. "Mercy's not kidding about laying down the law with this. None of them are."

"Figured that."

"Are you going to be okay?"

"Do I have a choice?"

"If you didn't, we wouldn't be allowed at Bertha's—we both know that."

"So you're not going to get in trouble for this?" Linc asked.

"Of course I am. So what else's new?"

Linc snorted. "Ditto."

"So, you have fun tonight?" Rush asked cautiously, his subtle way of feeling Linc out about the Mercy-cheating thing. It's not like it wasn't on his mind, but knowing it and talking about it were two different things entirely.

Was it considered cheating if Mercy thought Linc had left him? It was a hard thing to wrestle with, considering where Linc had been during that time.

Still, he answered honestly with, "It was a good time."

Would've been better still if he wasn't forcing himself not to panic about Project X and Heathens, because panic wouldn't solve shit. Talking to Castle about it? That just might.

"You and Vann had fun." Rush shot him a side glance.

"Is there a question there?"

"C'mon, Linc—spill."

"He's not going to touch me. Havoc rules."

"But those don't apply to kissing Jethro."

"Fucking Christ—Havoc is worse than a hen party." Linc shook his head. "For the record, Jethro kissed me."

"But you didn't stop him," Rush pointed out.

"No, I didn't. And why do you ask questions you already know the answers to?"

"I learned it by watching you." Rush cackled. "But seriously . . . do you want it to get back to Mercy?"

"What I want in relation to Mercy doesn't seem to matter."

"Sorry, man." Rush looked concerned. "But he's gonna flip when he finds out."

"Good. Let him."

"I think . . . he's trying to do the right thing?"

"Did Ryker tell you to say that?"

"Ryker explained that he claimed me too. I just didn't realize it."

"You and Ryker were totally different, man." Linc rubbed his forehead. "I don't want to talk about this anymore."

"Need me as your alibi?" Rush asked as they entered Havoc, with a wave to the men at the gate as they breezed by.

"Nah, I'm sneaking in," Linc assured him. "Might as well let him think I'm doing what he's wanting me to do."

Rush sighed. "You never used to be this stubborn."

"Shit changes."

"I know, Linc. I do." Rush glanced over at him, looking so damned concerned in the low light on the dash as the car continued to barrel along the Havoc roads. They were close now. "Tell me what's going through your head. Please. I want to help."

Linc didn't want anyone inside his head. "It's cool, Rush. Swear. I'm just frustrated, that's all."

Rush rolled his eyes. "Tell me something I don't know."

CHAPTER 13

FEELS JUST LIKE I'M WALKING ON BROKEN GLASS

Linc snuck in craftily and silently. Rush had offered to text Mercy to say that Linc was staying with him that night, but hell, they'd both already pushed their luck.

It's not like Rush wasn't under the same kind of orders as Linc. Rush wasn't exactly a probie member, but he was still being protected as if he were. Which meant Havoc thought he was vulnerable as hell.

It was part of the reason he'd jumped at Castle's job offer in the first place—after being watched over by Bram all those years, Linc realized that, at some point, he'd have to take over for himself. The Army had helped with that, but Castle's training had tipped it over the edge.

Finally, Linc was inside, shoes off, padding silently through the house.

The empty house, because after all that sneaking, Mercy wasn't even home. The bed hadn't been slept in, Linc's water was still on the counter exactly where he'd left it, and nothing else had been bothered. There was no note, no message on Linc's phone. *Nothing.*

It was two in the morning, and while it seemed ridiculous (okay, it was) for Linc to be pissed at him for not being there . . . Linc was.

He sat on the couch. Texted Rush to ask if Ryker was home and got a disgruntled *No. WTF* text in response.

Club business?

Who knows? was Rush's reply. But Rush knew Ryker was coming home to him. *For* him.

Linc was just some kind of transient, owned, money-owing guest. He called Bram, who answered groggily, "What's wrong?"

"You're old, that's what. Two in the morning on a Saturday, you should be up and out. Or at least fucking someone," Linc told him sourly.

Bram sighed. "Linc, do you need me to come over?"

"No, forget it," he sighed, especially after hearing rustling in the background and Sweet's deep voice rumbling.

"Sure?"

"Yeah. It's just . . . Mercy's not home."

"Oh." More rustling and Linc rolled his eyes as he pictured his brother and Sweet mouthing this conversation to each other.

"It's nothing. I was just hoping he . . . I mean, everything was okay. I didn't know if it was club business." He paused. "Forget it. God, I'm pathetic."

"I'm coming over."

"No."

"With food. Give me twenty." Bram hung up, and, in response, Linc's stomach growled.

"Asshole," he told it.

Bram was as good as his word, bringing in burgers, fries, and shakes from the diner and walking in without knocking. He assessed Linc with a quick once-over, and Linc had long ago stopped trying to hide things from his brother—at least not too hard.

But Bram kept the conversation light until the food was unpacked and they'd sat down. It was only once they'd started eating that he told Linc, "Mercy kept your concert shirt . . . until I stole it back."

He reached into another bag he'd brought in that Linc hadn't noticed and tossed the shirt over.

"I was wondering where it went to." He hadn't realized how much he'd missed it until he felt the soft as anything fabric. It was a Motörhead T-shirt, old as fuck, perfectly broken in. It'd been from Linc's first concert. Bram had taken him, and this shirt represented all the good things in Linc's life. His talisman.

"I had it when we were looking for you," Bram admitted. "Mercy left it for me when I first came to Havoc. He used it as proof that I was who I said I was."

Linc frowned. "Like a test?"

Bram nodded. "We got into a fight about it. I might've punched him. A few times."

"Would've paid to see that."

"He was hurting. Bad. I didn't see it at the time. Actually, not until that night. I accused him of sitting on his ass and he . . ." Bram shook his head. "He was hurt. I know he should've looked for you but . . . he really thought you'd just up and left him."

Linc's face felt hot, and he immediately lost his appetite. He took a deep swallow of the fountain soda, played with the straw to avoid answering. Problem was, it didn't stop him from feeling.

"Linc? Talk to me."

But Linc didn't know what the hell to say. The Heathens had been after him for revenge against Mercy, and they would've found him no matter what. But for now, it sounded like it was all a big misunderstanding. That'd be fine and easy enough to fix if what happened hadn't happened. But it had. He'd been attacked because they knew he belonged to Mercy. And Mercy hadn't come to get him for the exact opposite reason—because he didn't think Linc thought of himself as his. Beyond that . . .

"There are a lot of secrets," he told Bram. "Mainly Mercy's. And they're not secrets anymore, but they came out because of me, and I swear he's pissed about that."

Bram didn't tell him that he was wrong or crazy—he never did that. Linc might drive him crazy on a regular basis, but Bram always allowed him to express his feelings without fear. He'd make a great dad. He really would. Even still slightly messed up—because PTSD didn't just go away—Bram gave the best advice. "I don't know what to do, Bram."

"He's got you here."

"Because it's protocol. A way to keep me safe so he doesn't need to feel any guiltier. I refuse to be anyone's guilt trip."

"Did you ask him?"

"Not sure I want to hear the answer. Besides, you're the one who always told me not to ask a question I didn't already know the answer to."

"Actually, it was 'don't meet someone you don't already know,' but it's nice to know you listen. And I'm sorry you're feeling shitty. Do you want me to talk to Mercy—"

"Fuck no. God. No."

Bram laughed. "Just checking. Hey, I'd be subtle."

"As a train wreck. I just think there's too much between us. Sometimes that makes things unfixable."

"I think it's too soon to give up."

Linc changed the subject. "Are you going to stay in the ATF?"

"In light of what's happening with the Kill Devils and Heathens . . . I could do something like Jethro."

"Yeah. But Casey doesn't rush off to save Jethro. I'm not sure Sweet can say the same thing."

Bram pointed at him as he chewed. His way of saying *point taken*.

"Jethro says I'd be good at undercover work," Linc said casually, sending out feelers, but Bram half choked just the same.

"I will kill that fucker."

"You don't think I'd be good?"

"I didn't say that." Bram stared at him. "Is it really what you want to do?"

"Honestly? Maybe." He sat back and played with the straw. "Does Mercy know I sneak out?"

"Yes."

"So everyone at Bertha's is watching me?"

"Kind of."

"Great."

"It's not like he's telling them. Actually, they love it that you sneak out. They're just watching you the same way they always watch Rush."

"So they think Mercy doesn't know?"

"I don't think they think about that." Bram frowned. "They're just happy to see you acting like you."

Linc took that in, because he really didn't feel like himself, but it was good to know. Maybe he was slowly turning back into his old self.

But Mercy was far from his old self. Instead, he seemed to be re-creating himself, turning into a Havoc enforcer, a brutal man to those who crossed him.

To those he liked and respected? He was reserved. And to most of his conquests, he'd effectively turned off the part of himself that could get hurt.

Linc needed a key, but hell, he'd settle for a case of TNT. Or a brick of C4.

Whether him kissing Jethro would be enough to blow the lid off Mercy remained to be seen.

"How are you really doing?" Bram pressed.

"I'm . . ." *All right. Better. Needing to be touched. Shitty.* "Fine."

"That's the way I used to answer." Bram gave him a worried smile. "I'm here, Linc."

"You always are," Linc assured him.

CHAPTER 14

TENDER IS THE NIGHT

It was four thirty in the morning and Mercy still wasn't home. Linc had sent Bram back to Sweet half an hour ago. Now, still wide-awake and getting more pissed off by the second, he went in search of Mercy . . . on the compound, though. Because he wasn't stupid enough to go off-site on his own.

There were a few places Mercy could be, and Linc started with the clubhouse. Technically, he needed to go inside with a Havoc member, but he figured that wouldn't be an issue.

It was more crowded than he'd thought. A lot of the guys who'd been at Bertha's had moved the party over here, and there were a good number of guests here as well.

Tug was there. Boomer too, and both moved to greet him, or maybe shield him, but it was an enthusiastic greeting nonetheless.

Neither man mentioned Mercy, but Mercy wasn't here. As crowded as it was, Linc could still see that.

"Did you come here looking for anyone in particular?" Tug asked finally.

"Don't mean to take you away." Linc motioned to the pretty woman who'd been sitting on Tug's lap when Linc had come in.

"Cassie? She's an old friend."

Linc snorted. "Right. But yeah, Mercy wasn't home and . . ." *And he's avoiding me.*

"I'm sure he's fine. Being an enforcer's a busy job," Tug attempted to reassure him.

"You're an enforcer," Linc pointed out.

"It's my night off?" Tug tried, and Linc figured they all knew Mercy was avoiding him, the way they all knew Mercy was letting him sneak out.

"Go back to Cassie. I'm tired. I'm past my bedtime." Linc smiled and headed out into the cool night air. He walked up the hill, hoping it would clear his mind, or at least make him tired enough to actually sleep.

But when he got back to the house and climbed the wooden steps, Mercy was sitting on the porch. "Heard you're looking for me." His legs were propped up on the railing. "Didn't realize I had a curfew."

"You don't," Linc said carefully, not liking Mercy's tone of voice. It was cold. Angry. He flashed back to his time in that cell and tried not to shiver. "I was just worried."

Mercy stood abruptly, his boots dropping with a heavy thud to the wooden planks, loud enough to make Linc jump. "You don't need to be. If you want to go to the clubhouse, that's fine. But not if you ask where I am."

"Why? Does it make you look bad in front of your brothers?" *Dangerous territory, Linc. Slow it down.*

"Yes," Mercy said. "Claiming you means that you're mine. Rules don't apply the other way around. Tried giving you a long leash but that doesn't seem to be working—for me or for Havoc. Because you're out there, fucking around."

"But you fucking other guys while I was locked in a basement is cool—with you and Havoc?" Linc asked, unable to keep his tone anything but biting. "Is that why you were giving me a long leash—figured if you let me screw around, we'd be even?"

Mercy stared daggers at him.

"Fuck that and fuck you—I'm not your MC bitch." Linc went to walk off the porch, but Mercy caught him by the arm.

"Thought that was what you wanted, Linc. Ever hear the phrase, 'be careful what you wish for'?"

"I didn't wish for you to screw around on me."

"I thought you left me. Make no mistake, baby—it's not a regular thing. Not since you've been back."

"Even though you can?"

"Even though," Mercy agreed, his tone softer. "That why you let Jethro kiss you?"

"I need you, Mercy. I need you with me, okay?"

"Thought you'd never ask."

"You really thought I didn't need you there?"

Mercy shrugged. "I think you need to follow orders. Directions."

Linc laughed, tried to anyway, but it came out hollow. Nerves tightening his belly. "It, ah, won't happen again?"

"Now why don't I believe that?" Mercy's voice was a rough silk that slid down Linc's back, making him hard—harder still, as Mercy moved in closer. "I asked a question."

Linc felt lightheaded as the heat from Mercy's body radiated over him. It'd been so damned long since he'd had a tender touch . . . would it be longer still? Was this all a goddamned tease? "Fuck your questions, Mercy, and fuck you trying to scare me. Just touch me."

If Mercy was surprised by the demand, he didn't let on. He remained inches away and Linc fisted his own hands to stop himself from reaching out first. "What is it, Mercy? Am I too dirty for you now?"

Mercy's answer was an immediate, "Never," in a barely there rasp. His hands moved to snake down the back of Linc's neck, and Linc leaned into the contact, rubbing his cheek against Mercy's inner wrist like a cat. Seeking attention. Affection. Friction.

"Please." He hated begging, but this small touch was so good. Wanted.

Needed.

It'd taken him a while to get to this point. At first, he hadn't wanted to see Mercy, when he was angry at everything and everyone. But he'd suddenly gone from zero to sixty with no in-between. His body was hot. Feverish. His skin was too tight and itchy. He had to get out of his clothes, needed to palm his cock and come.

Fuck it. He brought his hands to his pants and unzipped. His dick was so goddamned hard it hurt and he caught it, stroked it, all as Mercy stayed still but remained touching him.

A strangled groan escaped his throat and Mercy's expression softened. Linc's breath hitched and he began to sway slightly, but was steadied by Mercy's touch.

He wanted to close his eyes but he refused to break Mercy's gaze. He didn't care that Mercy wasn't stroking his cock.

"Good, Linc," Mercy said just then. "Faster. You need this."

Linc didn't bother to bite back his groans. "What do you need, Mercy? Tell me."

Mercy's mouth opened and his Adam's apple bobbed from a hard swallow before he let go of Linc.

And sank to his knees.

Linc stopped stroking in surprise but it didn't matter, because Mercy moved his hand and took Linc into his mouth.

"Fuck," Linc cried out, his body shuddering as Mercy sucked, wet and hot.

His hands carded in Mercy's hair, then gripped as his orgasm threatened and there was no way to hold it back. "Don't stop—please."

Mercy just sucked him harder, his tongue flicking along Linc's cock while still managing to swallow him down. And then Linc shot . . .

He was yelling, mixing *Mercy* and *fuck* and *yes*, and he was surprised that no one came to interrupt. Because if this was a goddamned dream? He didn't want to wake up.

Finally, his knees began to shake and Mercy stood and gathered him, pulled him close and herded him into the house . . . and up the stairs and into their bed.

He stripped Linc. Linc's head felt heavy and his body light from the climax. Mercy seemed to instinctively know that. Babied him. Tucked him in. But Linc held tight to him, not letting him leave.

Mercy took his cut off and placed it reverently on the chair. Havoc men treated their rockers with the upmost respect. But Mercy's clothes were another matter, at least once he stripped himself of weapons—Linc would remember this later—the guns, knives, knuckles. But now, he was just impatient. And hard again.

Finally, Mercy was naked, his abs cut and chiseled. Tanned and tattooed. Mercy was a beautiful man—all-American beauty gone rough. His face held the scruff from several days and his hair was longer and blond. He was tangled with intricate ink running up and down both arms, chest, back, and a thigh. Linc had once spent time licking the patterns while Mercy watched.

But that was then. This?

Like their first time.

No. Like Linc's first time. He was needy, nervous, intense. "C'mon, Mercy, don't make me beg."

Toward the end of his captivity, he'd stopped begging for anything in that basement of Heathens' Clubhouse, not for Mercy or mercy—at least not out loud. Maybe it'd made things worse, pissed them off more since they seemed to like his pleading, but that's what he'd done. It's what he'd used to do at home too, when he was younger: he could only take so much before he'd lose himself and Bram would attract the attention away and take the beatings.

Mercy moved closer now, his hands on either side of Linc's shoulders, and Linc leaned up and wrapped his arms around Mercy's back, pulling them chest-to-chest. Put his lips to Mercy's and kissed him, and after a few seconds, Mercy was kissing him back. Taking over the kisses, and they became demanding, punishing, and so damned good.

"Touch me. All over," Linc murmured against his mouth.

"Demanding, aren't we?"

"You used to—" Suddenly, the words caught on Linc's tongue, because he didn't know what the truth was anymore. "Forget it."

Mercy backed off slowly, his eyes on Linc. "What just happened?"

"I don't know anything anymore. Where I stand with you. Where I ever did. Was it all a lie?"

"You can't . . . you doubt . . ." Mercy stopped. "Fuck. Of course you do."

"You think ordering me around is going to keep me from running?"

"No," Mercy told him quietly. "It's going to show you that you're wanted."

Linc's breath quickened, because he'd never thought about it that way. "I thought . . . I'm an obligation."

"I don't fuck my obligations, baby." Mercy surged forward and pressed him back against the mattress, covering Linc's body with his. He held Linc's arms over his head, catching Linc's wrists in one hand and alternately punishing his nipples with his teeth and tongue, laving and tweaking until they were hard and sensitive. Until Linc fought for breath between his groans.

Mercy was watching him carefully, no doubt to make sure that holding him down didn't freak him out. And no, this was different. So different, because Mercy would let him up if he asked.

But he didn't, instead telling Mercy, "More. I need more."

"We're getting there," Mercy assured him. "Trust me." Linc nodded, because he did, and Mercy sat back on his heels. "I'm going to spread you . . . lick you. And you'll want me to stop, but I won't."

He got up then, went to his discarded jeans and freed his belt . . . and walked back to the bed. Linc's cock twitched when he realized what Mercy was going to do, and Mercy chuckled softly. Then he knelt between Linc's legs and, as Linc watched, he leaned forward and wrapped the leather band around Linc's wrists, tying them together and ultimately to the headboard.

The fact that it was leather and not chains, and that it was tight enough to restrain him but he could escape if he needed to, made it that much easier to bear . . . and that much harder. It was a different feeling, a totally new sensation.

He couldn't help but stare up at his bound wrists and then again at Mercy. "I'm not going to want you to stop. It's been too long."

"Been a while for me too," Mercy told him as he pressed their bodies together, and Linc felt Mercy's bare cock throbbing against his. He bucked his hips up, enjoying the friction.

His skin was tight. Hot. His earlier orgasm had taken the edge off but barely. The relief was more about finally having real contact with Mercy—that he hadn't pulled away from him under the guise of "For Linc's own good."

Linc swallowed, hard, as Mercy began to trace Linc's skin with his tongue, working his way down Linc's neck and chest, nipping, biting, worshipping. He looked at Linc like he was brand fucking new.

He sucked on a nipple and fingered the other, rolling it, putting enough delicious pressure on both so that they stung, and then he soothed with his mouth. "We need to pierce these. So fucking sensitive already and then they'll be even more so."

"God . . . Mercy." It came out somewhere between a prayer and a plea as Mercy continued to play his body expertly.

Mercy grinned up at him. "Love how much you need the dirty talk."

"So do you," Linc shot back and was rewarded with fingers brushing his balls and rubbing the sensitive strip of flesh behind them.

"Baby likes that," Mercy murmured before moving down to put his face between Linc's legs and replace his fingers with his tongue. Linc gasped and bucked and then Mercy's hands went to his hips, centering him. Grounding him. He wanted Mercy to hold him hard enough to leave bruises, marking him. Erasing everyone else from his mind.

Mercy palmed his cock and the slow squeeze and slide, coupled with Mercy's rimming, was making Linc incoherent.

And then Mercy was reaching up to unhook Linc from the headboard, turning him onto his elbows and knees and rubbing his cock against Linc's ass. He felt the cold lube being worked inside of him, along with two of Mercy's fingers, and he pushed back against them, hissing at the sudden fullness . . . knowing it was nothing compared to Mercy's cock but wanting it all just the same.

Finally, Mercy was behind him. "Going to fuck you now, baby. Fuck you incoherent."

Linc's body fought to accept the intrusion as Mercy pushed his cock forward inside of him. The pain gave way to a long, slow burn that raced up his spine and spread, flooding his entire body like an uncontrolled fire. His dick was throbbing, hanging heavy between his legs as Mercy pulsed inside of him. He slid all the way in, his balls touching Linc's ass, and then he reared forward so he hit Linc's prostate.

Linc saw stars. Cries fell from his mouth, begging Mercy to "do that again, now." And Mercy pulled back and did what he asked, but in a maddeningly slow way that had Linc on edge, desperately trying to fuck himself on Mercy's dick.

Mercy wouldn't let him though, was completely controlling the fuck. "Baby, if it's too much for you . . ."

"It's not. Don't stop."

"Oh, I wasn't planning on it," Mercy assured him. And he made good on his word, began to hammer inside of Linc, taking him to the brink of his orgasm and then pulling back with shallow strokes that had Linc sweating, whimpering. "Jesus, Linc . . . so fucking gorgeous like this. Taking me all in."

Mercy made it so the only thing Linc could focus on was him, his cock, the thrum of his pulse . . . the raw, molten need that took him over completely. Mercy was leaning over him, biting his back and shoulders as he tortured Linc with a slow, steady grind. He tugged Linc's hair, twisted his neck so he could kiss him, long and deep. And only then did he release Linc's hair and go to work, pounding inside of him with the strokes that Linc needed, letting Linc meet him at the upstroke so Mercy nailed his gland each and every time he drove inside of him.

"Mercy, I'm . . ." The words barely dropped out of his mouth before he was coming, all over his chest, the bed, without any contact on his cock but air. The climax hung there, trapping him in its waves of pleasure, tightening his body with an intensity he couldn't recall feeling before.

Mercy held him tight, making sure not to let him go as his orgasm made him feel like he was falling out of the sky.

Linc woke in Mercy's arms. He blinked and tried to process what was happening, but it was like his brain was trying to slog through thick syrup.

"'S'okay, babe," Mercy murmured. "Just a bad dream. You're safe. Try to drift back to sleep."

He wanted to ask if Mercy would keep holding him because the contact was the only good thing to come out of it. But instead he nuzzled against Mercy's bare chest like he wasn't ever planning on leaving. Because he wasn't. "Sorry I woke you."

"Nothing to be sorry about."

"Kissing Jethro . . . wanted it to be you but you won't come near me . . . unless I'm screaming in my sleep." Linc knew he was babbling now, but he didn't care, because he'd finally had the courage to say it. "Need you to kiss me, Mercy."

Mercy stroked his hair and rocked him. Linc wanted to protest, but it was nice. Safe.

And then Mercy leaned in and kissed him and it was fucking perfect. Linc got hard but he was too damned sleepy to act on it. No, the kiss was enough.

"Sleep, baby. I'll be here when you wake." Mercy's voice rumbled in his chest as he drifted off, and he wasn't sure if Mercy really spoke those words or if Linc just wanted to hear them so badly that he convinced himself Mercy had.

CHAPTER 15

HAIR OF THE DOG

Mercy let Linc sleep in the next morning. He'd gotten up and showered, more nervous than anything that Linc would wake with regrets.

Mercy? Had none. Except there was still so much between them. Secrets they both knew about the other but that they hadn't spoken out loud . . . and they needed to spill them out on the table between them, hash through them. Linc especially. Mercy wasn't fooled that Linc was healed—not on the inside. PTSD was a royal bitch, and it was going to come roaring back and bite them in the ass no matter how good things were at the moment.

Finally, sometime after eleven in the morning, Linc woke and rolled over. He looked between Mercy, who was sitting in the chair by the window and the clock. "Shit—the shop . . ."

"It'll keep. Take your time—Tug's there now, and I'll drop you off when you're ready. After you have breakfast."

He watched as Linc nodded, stretched, looking content. "Thanks."

"And then, after work, we'll head over to the bar."

Linc was halfway out of bed, stopped, and frowned. "We're going to Bertha's . . . together?" he asked hesitantly.

"Worried it won't be fun with me there?"

"Just the opposite," Linc said quietly, so seriously that Mercy wanted to take him home instead and refuse to share him with the world. But no, tonight was important, for both of them.

He also had to kill Jethro as well, so it would be killing two birds with one very bloody stone.

"Why are you smiling?" Linc asked suspiciously.

"I'm not allowed to smile?"

"I'm beginning to realize Havoc men only smile like that when they're imagining mayhem."

Later, after Tug brought Linc back home, sometime after eight in the evening, Linc changed and ate dinner.

"Still up for going out?" Mercy asked.

"Um, if you are?" Linc said hesitantly. "I mean, are you?"

"You're very suspicious."

"I'm just . . ."

"Used to sneaking out?" Mercy finished.

Linc smirked. "Little bit, yeah."

Mercy slung an arm around him. "I'd love to take the bikes, but I think the truck's our best bet, yes?"

As he spoke, Tug pulled his truck up outside the house. Vann, Boomer, and Shaman were behind him with their bikes.

"Sweet and Bram are meeting us there," Mercy told him, once they were in the truck and driving toward Bertha's. "Rush and Ryker too."

"A regular party," Linc murmured. "Any Hangmen going to be there?"

Mercy shrugged and tried to look innocent, but he had as much chance of that as the devil did.

Linc just rolled his eyes.

They got to Bertha's relatively quickly, especially because Tug drove like a maniac on a good day, and was blasting the music, which kept the conversation down. Mercy kept a hand on Linc's thigh the entire ride, which had Linc feeling revved up by the time they arrived at Bertha's.

It was still early, so the volume wasn't at ear-splitting levels when they walked inside, but the crowds were already swelling around the bar and the dance floor. Linc caught sight of Rush and Ryker, swore he caught a glance of Jethro as well.

"I'm going to get drinks. Grab a table," Mercy told him.

Linc bit his lip to stop a snide comment about being allowed to go get a table alone and headed to the back to snag one.

Vann followed, sat next to him, and leaned in. "I think Mercy should beat the shit out of Jethro for touching you."

"You didn't tell him that, did you? Tell me you didn't." Linc groaned and pressed his fingers to his temples.

"So you want me to lie to you?"

"Fuck me."

"That's what I told Mercy to do," Vann said triumphantly.

"You were raised by fucking wolves," Linc muttered. "Deranged."

"I didn't think that would be a problem for you."

Linc snorted. "It's not." Then he heard shouts from over by the dance floor. Mercy's voice—then Jethro's, although he couldn't make out actual words. "Shit, they're going to fight."

"Nothing you can do to stop it," Vann reasoned.

Mercy clocked Jethro the second he'd walked into Bertha's, which was why he'd sent Linc to get a table. Because he had no doubt Linc would try to break up any fight, and Mercy needed to punch Jethro without interference.

Jethro met him halfway, and they stopped, inches from each other.

"Heard you're looking for me, Mercy."

"I'm going to wipe that fucking smile off your face," Mercy told him.

"You can try."

"Linc's mine. I claimed him."

"I'm not Havoc so I don't follow your fucking rules." Jethro sneered.

Mercy was aware that a small crowd had formed around them. The bouncers wouldn't stop their fight, but would make sure that no innocents got hurt in the melee. "He's mine."

"Really doesn't seem like you're interested" was Jethro's response.

"He doesn't seem too interested in you either, if all you got was a kiss." Jethro seemed completely unconcerned that Mercy knew about the kiss, and Mercy wasn't sure which of those pissed him off more.

"He needed you. You weren't there," Jethro told him with brutal honesty.

"And you were going to step in and save him?"

"If you didn't man up, yeah."

Mercy nodded calmly, then caught Jethro on the jaw with a left hook. Jethro stumbled back and then reared forward, and the two men locked together, fueled by the yells of the crowd. Mercy threw several punches, including a direct hit to Jethro's solar plexus, which had the man sucking wind for several minutes.

"You fucker," Jethro growled and grabbed him. "You weren't fucking him. I hope to hell you are now."

Mercy pushed back and swung, hitting Jethro's jaw and splitting his lip . . . fully aware that he was far more angry at himself than he was at Jethro. Maybe that's why he let Jethro get a few punches in before Sweet and Casey were separating them.

"Not good for business," Sweet admonished him.

"Fuck you for enjoying that so much," Mercy shot back. "You smug bastard."

Sweet didn't bother denying it. "Come on, I'll buy you a drink."

"You own the place. Asshole."

Still, Mercy came away from the fight satisfied that he'd gotten his message across, and he figured that Jethro felt the same.

But it was easy for Jethro and Vann to tell him to take care of Linc, to fuck him, to touch him, when they didn't know.

Mercy knew. He understood what Linc was dealing with . . . because even though it hadn't happened to him, he'd been a Heathen and he knew their operations firsthand. All of them.

It wasn't beneath him to admit that he'd fucked up in the beginning. He should've moved Linc back to Havoc immediately, shouldn't have been so invested in his own mourning that he left Linc in pain.

Linc had been with Bram, and Mercy knew that the brothers needed each other.

But Linc had also needed you. And that was painfully apparent.

Mercy cut through the quickly dispersing crowd to find Linc, who was waiting for him, standing by himself. When Linc saw him, his countenance changed—nervous and yet somehow still seemingly eager, and when Mercy got close, he slid his hand around the back of Linc's neck. "You good, baby?"

"Did you kill Jethro?"

"We came to a mutual understanding. Nothing for you to worry about." Mercy felt calm. His knuckles were scraped and he'd have a hell of a bruise on his cheek, but Jethro would have more.

Linc looked around him. "Well, Jethro's still here . . . and he's smiling . . . so I'm guessing no bad blood?"

"Not unless you're going to kiss him anytime I'm not around to watch you?"

"No. And it didn't mean anything. And it's not about being watched." Linc attempted to shrug it off.

Mercy stared into Linc's worried eyes and took control of the situation. "We're not doing this."

"We're not . . . arguing?"

"Not in front of other people."

Linc frowned and he looked fucking adorable. Probably because he'd already had tequila. And then a light dawned behind his eyes. "Because I'm yours."

"That's exactly right. You need to get used to the idea."

"Which entails doing exactly what you say and fuck whatever I might need." But there was no fire behind Linc's words.

"What do you need?" Mercy demanded. "Because for this, you need to tell me. Sneaking out tells me you want to be chased. So I made sure I'm here."

Linc nodded. "You know what I want."

"You want everything to be the same as it was. And you also know it won't be. You need to be handled and I can handle you. I will handle you—you need to trust in that."

"I'm trying," Linc said softly.

"I know, baby. You're inside out."

"So are you."

Mercy gave him a small smile. "I'm not who you need to worry about."

"You're here because I told you I needed you here—"

"Yes."

"But you ignored me when I told you to stay away."

Mercy muttered, "I respected your wishes. You didn't know I was there."

Linc was staring at him insolently . . . which was also goddamned fucking sexy. And the look got more so when Mercy grabbed him and half dragged him outside into the alley.

"Mercy, my jacket's still inside," Linc told him, but stopped when Mercy pinned him to the brick wall with his body, put a hand inside Linc's loose cargos and caught his cock in his warm palm.

Linc wound an arm around Mercy's shoulders and kissed him. Yeah, Linc wasn't feeling any pain at all, his grin easy, and he was still dancing, but he was only dancing for Mercy now.

"I want you dancing on my cock," Mercy told him.

"Right out here? Where everyone can watch?"

"You'd do it. Out here, in there. If I made you spread yourself on the bar." Mercy stroked Linc harder, and Linc's breath quickened. "Totally naked. Everyone watching. Maybe I'll let anyone who wants to take a turn."

Linc groaned. "But you'd be there, right?"

"Right next to you, baby. Holding you open."

It moved him that Linc needed to make sure, even in the fantasy, that Mercy was there . . . that he wanted Mercy there with him.

"I have no control over my body when you're around," Linc practically growled.

"That works for me." Mercy took his hand out of Linc's pants and ran his thumb over the pulse point on Linc's neck and Linc's breathing hitched just from that simple contact. "You don't seem to be having a problem with it."

"I crave you. Trust me, it's a problem."

Mercy obviously didn't share his concern, just leaned in and sucked the pulse point he'd just stroked, hard. "Bet I can make you come before Rush comes."

Linc strained to look over Mercy's shoulder and saw that Rush and Ryker were down the alley and across from them, and they were damned close to fucking out in the open. When Linc looked back at him, Mercy was grinning at that before turning his full attention to Linc.

Linc shivered, anticipation more than anything, and the sense of relief that followed Mercy and Jethro being okay after their fight make him hard. "How much . . . and how far are you going?"

Mercy frowned and Linc repeated, "How much? You said you'd bet money."

Mercy smiled. "A grand."

"Big spender." Linc grinned back as Mercy's hand began to play between his legs again. "How far?"

"You want more than a handjob, baby?" Mercy's voice was wicked. "Want me to bend you over and fuck you? Bring you inside and do it?"

Linc groaned as Mercy worked his cock in his calloused palm. "Not fair."

"The dirty talk's one of your favorite parts. So's the follow-through."

Linc wrapped a hand around the back of Mercy's neck and kissed him, because he needed to be kissed. It was like Mercy was his lifeline . . . because he was, and he kissed Linc like he'd never let him go.

Linc kissed him back the exact same way, until they were both out of breath, and Linc was frantic with need. He couldn't get close enough and Mercy seemed to instinctively understand.

That made Linc's need stronger. Hungrier. He wanted to wrap around Mercy completely and let him do whatever the hell he wanted to, bets be damned.

"Want to take a ride back to Havoc . . . or find someplace more private along the way?" Mercy asked. "Or I could invite Jethro back here . . . show him what he's missing."

"Fuck." Linc closed his eyes and leaned his forehead against Mercy's leather-clad shoulder. Mercy unzipped his cargos and freed his cock and began to stroke, and fuck, this wasn't fair. Between Mercy's hot, talented mouth sucking and marking his neck, and watching Ryker press against Rush in the dark, Mercy was going to win his bet with no problem.

Rush wasn't bothering to be quiet. He never was, and that wouldn't have changed whether he'd been alone with Ryker in the alley or not.

Mercy's fingers slid along his slit, pressing, milking, forcing a muffled groan from Linc's throat that echoed through the alley. "I'm going to lose the bet."

"Does it matter?"

"No," Linc murmured. Because the only thing that did was feeling Mercy against him as he came, hot and hard, his breath catching. "What you do to me . . ."

Mercy's free hand tightened behind his neck. "What you do to *me*."

Linc looked up and met his eyes. For a second, Linc was sure they'd never been closer . . . until they heard bottles breaking and shouts.

As the backdoor opened, Mercy immediately went on alert, his hand going to his weapon, his body covering Linc protectively. But it was just Boomer, his hands up, knowing full well he'd have weapons aimed at him.

"Pagans," was all he said before disappearing back inside.

Ryker and Rush were already zipping up and walking over toward them.

"I've got a weapon," Rush confirmed.

Mercy glanced at Linc. "I'll stay with you."

"No. You do your job," Linc told him, although he wanted nothing more than to keep Mercy safe. "Go protect. I'll stick with Rush."

Mercy dusted his knuckles across Linc's cheek. "Thanks, baby. Let's get you inside first."

He let Mercy lead him into the bar. Ryker locked the back door behind them with the dead bolt and then Linc and Rush watched their men disappear into the crowd.

"I can help," Linc said finally.

"They've got it. We'll be in the way," Rush said, his tone telling Linc that they were both completely unconvinced of that. "We know we're their vulnerability."

"And that's never going to change?"

"Not when you love somebody." Rush stared out the window as the yelling got louder. "Cops'll be here soon. Maybe we should get the hell out of here."

Linc frowned. As much as he didn't want to deal with the cops before his court case, something felt off. He glanced at the side door and then looked toward the back as the sirens got louder. "Where's your car?"

"I'm right out back—along the wall," Rush confirmed. He was looking around, but there was no one to tell, no one to ask. It was pure confusion.

"Let's go." Linc led the way through the throngs of panicking people toward the back. That door was double bolted as well, although people were letting themselves out and a bouncer, Monster, was locking up behind them.

"You should both stay," Monster told them.

"He's got court in a couple of days. If this place gets raided—" Rush started, right before they heard a megaphone's whine and then, "This is the police. We're coming in. We need everyone inside to stand down and put their hands in the air."

"What the fuck," Linc muttered, but Monster was letting them out.

When they hit the air, Linc knew immediately that his gut had been right, but hell, he'd rather face Pagans than the cops right now. It helped to get rid of some of his rage as he snapped his fist against the cheek of the first man who tried to grab him, because no, this wasn't happening.

"Linc!" Rush called as he fought off two men.

"I've got the right," Linc called back, and he had two of them on the ground and was fighting off a third by the time Mercy slammed through the back doors.

"You both okay?" Mercy asked.

"We're good," Linc told him.

"Fine," Rush said as Ryker came around the corner from the alley. "I guess we've got to bolt?"

Rush went with Ryker and Linc with Mercy into Tug's truck that was waiting around the corner. A few of the men stayed behind to deal with the police and the Pagans, but Linc was glad Mercy wasn't one of them.

"It was a trap, wasn't it?" Linc asked once Tug was on the highway. The music was turned up a bit and Tug and Boomer were talking, leaving Linc and Mercy to have some privacy in the back seat.

"Looks to be."

Linc shifted. "They were trying to funnel me out the back." Mercy nodded, his jaw tight. "Look, I'm sorry we left but—"

"Don't. You were thinking about court, which was important. You didn't do anything wrong," Mercy told him, his voice low. "You were fantastic."

Linc flushed. "Thanks."

"You weren't helpless." Mercy brought his lips down on Linc's head. "I'm sorry if I've been making you feel like that."

"You were only trying to protect what you lo—" Linc stopped and said, "Me," quickly.

"What I love," Mercy murmured. "You."

Linc leaned against him, suddenly realizing how tired he actually was. He didn't want to think about traps and Pagans and all the shit he needed to look over his shoulder for. And so, for tonight, he didn't.

CHAPTER 16

EVERYBODY PLAY THE GAME

By eleven the next morning, Linc was in the bonds shop, going through files, and smiling for what felt like the first time in ages. His body ached pleasantly from the night before. Mercy had left earlier, but he'd woken Linc up first with a quiet "Morning, babe," and a lingering touch . . . and the sense of relief flooded him that Mercy didn't think the night before was a mistake.

Even just the small block of time he'd had with Mercy had cleared his mind, more than a little. Miles to go and all that shit, but still . . .

Tug was his escort for the day—he was helping Mercy out with running down skips until Mercy and Sweet decided if the bonds shop was moving closer to Havoc. Linc didn't think that was such a great idea because it meant more outside people near Havoc, but he'd kept that thought to himself.

Now, he worked alone, while Tug went across the street to grab breakfast, and with Shaman on the roof and god knew who in the back lot—as usual. Stopping that wouldn't happen and he realized that he wouldn't be able to concentrate on much of anything without backup.

He started with the cases that had court dates coming up this week, which, of course, included him. Looking over the old bond form he'd filled out, complete with Bram's forged signature and the fake bit about Bram owning his own home, made him snort.

At the time, it'd gotten him what he'd wanted and some that he hadn't, but in general, he didn't regret his call. But thinking about tomorrow, and the fact that the DA would no doubt try to press him to testify against the Heathens, made his head hurt. He quickly shoved his file aside and looked through the rest of the cases.

It would be a slow court week—just him and two other people. One, a teenage girl, would probably get off with a slap on the wrist for a shoplifting first offense, and the second? A low-level drug dealer who'd gotten caught by an undercover cop near the docks. It was a second offense, which carried jail time, unless he turned on his supplier. And the case was set for . . . an hour ago.

Linc paused and looked at the paperwork again. The man—Ty Larimer—should've had his court case two weeks earlier. His lawyer had gotten him a continuance.

What kind of public defender got a dealer a continuance? Linc ran the lawyer's name and bells started going off. Then he called Mercy's contact at the courthouse and discovered that Ty hadn't shown for court, his lawyer had begged off the case, and there was a warrant out for Ty's arrest.

Which meant Linc had to get to him first.

He texted Tug. *Need to visit a lawyer's office, then follow-up on a skip.*

He watched Tug stroll across the street and into the shop. "You know you're supposed to let Mercy handle the skips."

"C'mon, Tug. Give me a goddamned break." He picked up the file. "Let's go check his house . . . but first, I need to check in on his lawyer. He's along the way."

Tug looked like he wanted to argue, but instead, he held the door open for Linc, turned the sign to Closed and locked the door behind him. Linc climbed into the passenger's side of Tug's giant black truck and soon, Tug was headed toward the lawyer's office.

"What's got you cranked about this case?" Tug asked finally.

Linc frowned, pointed to the string of cases attached to the lawyer via Google. "How many two-bit drug pushers do you know that can afford a five-hundred-dollar-an-hour attorney?"

"Not many . . . unless they're cartel," Tug said thoughtfully. "You've got court tomorrow. Might not be the best day to fuck around with this?"

"Then let's not tell Mercy—and let's not get caught. This is just recon," Linc promised.

Next to him, Tug muttered something about "usually have tequila to smooth the bad decisions."

"I'm just going information gathering. Nothing crazy. I don't want to fuck up court." Or his newfound peace with Mercy, as tenuous as it was. "I don't want you to go past the building. Stop before turning onto the block."

Tug did so. No doubt he understood that Linc was stopping the cameras the lawyer had on his building from capturing Tug's license plate.

"What're you going to do, Linc?"

"I'm going to go in and make an appointment." It was almost one in the afternoon, but that didn't mean the guy was going out for lunch. He also had no court cases on his docket today, either—Linc had checked with a clerk he knew at the court. "You've got to stay here. You'll have eyes on me the whole way in. I'll text you from inside."

"Jesus Christ, no wonder Mercy mutters to himself all the time."

Linc slid out of the car before Tug could argue, leaving him to mutter to himself. The inner office area wasn't big but it was clean, with polished leather couches in the waiting area and a big walnut desk where a pretty secretary sat, smiling up at him.

Linc was lucky that his kidnapping case hadn't made the papers. He was still pretty well unknown in these parts, and he knew how to use his looks to his advantage. And right now, he needed an advantage.

"Hey, honey, how can I help you?" The secretary had a Southern drawl and she leaned forward on her elbows.

Linc smiled. "I'm looking for a lawyer. I hear Mr. Blanchard's the best."

"Sure are in the right place. I'm guessing you don't have an appointment but let me see what I can do?"

Linc was glad Tug remained outside, because a Havoc rocker wouldn't get him this kind of hand-off and, like his momma used to say, *"You don't get a second chance to make a first impression."*

Now, he told the secretary, "I'd really appreciate that. My brother's been running me around this state and I'm not all that familiar with the area."

She looked sympathetic, knocked on the door to Ken Blanchard's office, and came back out a few moments later. "He'll see you now—he's got a few minutes before his lunch meeting. I hope it's not big trouble for you."

"At least I'm in the right place." Linc went in and met the dark-suited Ken Blanchard, who looked just like his photo—tall, bald, and probably much more lethal than he appeared. With his clientele, Blanchard was most definitely carrying and trained in different kinds of self-defense. He'd been a cop too, in New York.

Now, Linc offered his hand to shake and Blanchard took it firmly. "I'm Linc. Thanks for seeing me on short notice."

"Sit. Tell me what you need."

Linc leaned forward on his elbows, lowered his voice. "I need some help with my brother."

"Family's a bitch." Ken Blanchard smiled conspiratorially.

"He's, ah, in trouble for some low-level dealing . . . and I think he's in trouble with Project X."

Blanchard frowned. "How'd he get involved with them?"

"Not sure."

"What makes you think he's in trouble?"

"He got arrested—he's out on bail now but he refuses to testify against them. The DA's pressuring him and . . ." Linc shook his head. "Look, I can't say I blame him for not wanting to. But otherwise, he's doing jail time."

Blanchard nodded. "You seem like a nice guy, so I'm going to give you some free advice. Let him do the time. Turning on Project X is a death sentence."

Linc went cold inside, mainly because of the scary as hell look on Blanchard's face, even though what the lawyer said wasn't untrue. He stood. "I appreciate your honesty."

Blanchard saw him to the door. Linc spent a minute thanking the secretary and saw Blanchard leave through a side exit.

"Hey, is there a bathroom I can use? I've got a three-hour trip back home," he said.

"Sure, right through the door on your right." She went back to typing, so it was apparent that she wasn't closing the office for lunch.

He went into the side door, slid into Blanchard's unlocked office, and rooted through the files on his desk. He'd spotted Ty's earlier, and now, he opened it and snapped pictures of every document in the file—all ten of them—before going out to the front and thanking the secretary.

Twenty minutes after going inside, Linc was back in Tug's car, heading toward the shop.

Tug checked his rearview as he pulled away from the curb. "I got a hinky feeling."

"That's why I had you wait down the street, out of camera line," Linc said.

"What did the lawyer say?" Tug asked.

"Nothing compared to what his files said." Linc held up his phone. "I've got to go through what I got, but I don't expect our skip back to court anytime soon."

"A dismissal?"

"Not the kind anyone wants."

Tug shook his head. "This isn't good news."

"Let me get past court tomorrow. Maybe this guy will show tomorrow." Linc shrugged and Tug rolled his eyes. "What? I'm an optimist."

"No—you're a realist," Tug assured him.

Linc stayed late at the bonds office, because the thought of going back to Mercy's and pacing around made him sweat. Just because he had court tomorrow didn't mean Mercy would have the night off patrols, and Linc knew that going out tonight wasn't an option.

Finally, Tug dropped him off before midnight, after they grabbed a very late dinner at the diner on Havoc's compound. It was crowded, with a lot of the MC guys stopping by to wish Linc good luck on his court appearance in the morning.

Bram came by and watched a movie with him and finally, sometime after two in the morning, Linc went upstairs to bed and fell asleep. His dreams were scattered, all over the map, from Mercy to Heathens to court and Castle . . . and just as he began to get that restless feeling he often did in his sleep, right before the throes of a nightmare took hold, he woke to Mercy's arms banding around him.

His body sagged in relief. "Hey."

"Didn't meant to wake you," Mercy murmured.

"Glad you did." Linc pushed back into him, forcing Mercy to spoon his body, thinking about how many nights he'd been wishing for this. "What time is it?"

"Close to five." Mercy brushed some hair off Linc's face. "Bad dreams?"

"They were getting there," Linc admitted.

Mercy's palm flattened against his chest. He planted a kiss on the back of Linc's neck. "Here now. Nothing's getting through me."

"Good." Linc believed that.

"Tug mentioned you met with Blanchard today."

"Tug's good at that shit."

Mercy moved closer, so there was no room between their bodies, ran his fingertip along Linc's jawline. "Heard you uncovered some paperwork. Heard you took chances maybe you shouldn't have."

"Are you going to punish me for that? Or is this just you trying to distract me from thinking about court?"

"Is it working?" Mercy asked as innocently as he could, and it came off wicked as hell. Which meant Linc got harder.

"Yes."

"And you need the distraction?"

"Yes."

"You're worried."

"Trying not to be," Linc said honestly.

"Tell me exactly what you need, baby."

Linc swallowed hard. Things weren't back to normal between them, but they were far more comfortable than they'd been only forty-eight hours earlier. Might as well go for broke. "You, Mercy. I need you . . . to make me do things. Dirty things."

"Good, Linc. Now strip yourself," Mercy instructed. "Because distraction first . . . and then punishment for putting yourself in danger."

Linc thought about disobeying that order so Mercy would tie him down, but he wasn't exactly sure he was truly ready for that step. So his T-shirt came off first, and then the sweats.

"No underwear. Easy access," Mercy noted. "And you thought about not-complying . . . just for a second."

"Yeah," Linc admitted.

"Sit on the chair. Spread your legs. Stroke yourself slowly, eyes on me."

Linc nodded and did as he was told, fully conscious of Mercy's eyes on him . . . pinning him. He caught his cock in his hand and began to stroke. Chills broke out over his body as Mercy's gaze intensified.

"I'm going to pierce your nipples," Mercy said matter-of-factly, and Linc's dick surged in his palm. "Fuck, I should tape this so you can see how gorgeous you look."

Linc groaned, low in his throat, hips rising slightly off the chair as he tugged.

"Taste yourself," Mercy directed him.

Linc swept a finger over his cockhead, catching the drip, and brought it to his mouth, just like Mercy had him do a few nights earlier . . . but this time, Mercy watched him doing it and hell yeah. So fucking dirty. Mercy got him.

"Tell me what you're thinking," Mercy instructed.

"That . . . you're watching me. Ordering me . . . and I can't not do what you say."

"You can, but then you'll end up over my knee for disobeying. Or maybe you'll end up there anyway."

Linc whimpered, spread his legs wider as the orgasm threatened, the familiar ache surging inside of him.

"Beautiful, Linc. God, people would pay good money to see this." Mercy's voice narrating made it hotter and more embarrassing, but in a good way.

"Not gonna last."

"Good. I want you to shoot all over yourself."

Linc did, his body stiffening as he came, white ropes across his belly and chest, covering his hand. His breath came fast.

And then he froze, and Mercy was kneeling between his legs, like he'd done the other night on the porch, cleaning him with his tongue.

Linc reached out tentatively and put his hand in Mercy's hair . . . expected the entire scene to dissolve in a puff of smoke.

But it didn't. Mercy's eyes met his, locked and loaded, and Linc whimpered, seeing this big, tattooed man kneeling before him.

Linc was vulnerable as fuck, but so was Mercy. Neither man pushed each other tonight . . . it was all about limits and pleasure and easy. Linc wanted harder and rougher—but deep in his soul he knew he wasn't there yet. Close, but for now, this was fucking perfect, the hot wet suck of Mercy's mouth dragging his cock. Mercy's cheeks hollowed out as he sucked and then swallowed Linc's cock . . . and he was stroking himself at the same time. Linc fisted Mercy's thick hair and arched back. There was no reason to control his orgasm, to stop himself, to slow it down . . . and he couldn't have, even if he'd tried. Mercy was too damned good at what he did.

When Mercy was done, he sat back on his heels, studying Linc, who felt lazy and satiated . . . and somehow, still aroused, because that was pretty much the way he always felt around Mercy. "You okay, baby?"

"Yeah."

Mercy frowned. "No, not yet. Almost, though. Come on." He helped Linc up and led him into the shower. With the water warm enough, Linc got in first, with Mercy following right behind him.

Carrying lube and condoms.

"Turn around," Mercy told him. Linc did as Mercy asked, and one of Mercy's coated fingers slid inside of him. "So tight. Is this only for me?"

Mercy hit his prostate with his knuckle and Linc could only moan his answer. So, of course, Mercy did it again and again, until Linc was practically fucking the tile wall, finally managing, "Yours, Mercy. My ass is all yours."

"Good boy," Mercy crooned, adding a second finger and then a third, impaling Linc with pleasure. And then he caught Linc around the waist and turned him, picked him up, forcing Linc to wrap his arms and legs around him, his back to the tiles.

"Yeah, come on, Mercy—fuck me hard."

Mercy's sheathed cock pushed inside, a hot burn at first that spread slowly through his body as Mercy slid in deeper, until he settled against Linc's gland. Mercy latched on to one of his nipples, and Linc arched his back, wanting more.

And Mercy gave it to him, driving in harder and harder, until Linc was panting and grabbing at Mercy's wet skin, until the only thing on his mind was the orgasm that tore through him like a tornado . . . and how much he loved being in Mercy's arms.

CHAPTER 17

SAME OLD SONG AND DANCE

After Mercy's distractions, Linc gave up on sleep completely and managed to eat some of the breakfast Mercy made him.

"I've got to head up and meet with Sweet and the lawyer about a few things before you get there," Mercy said. "Scheduled stuff, okay? Nothing for you to worry about."

Linc nodded. "Go—I'm fine. I'll meet you up there." Which was good, because Mercy had started to hover and Linc was already nervous enough about how his day in court would go.

He showered, dressed, and found Tug waiting outside for him. "Aren't you getting tired of being my chauffeur?"

"You'd do the same for me, no?" Tug asked, which gave Linc pause. Because no, he hadn't thought about it like that, was still in the *Why am I being babied?* mode . . . and Tug had reminded him that it was more of a *what brothers do for one another* thing. Which made it better.

Another one of the layers lifted off him and floated away. "Yeah, I would, Tug."

Tug grinned and shot up the hill to the clubhouse, where Sweet and one of Havoc's lawyers was waiting in Sweet's office.

Sweet greeted Linc when he walked in, gesturing to the woman standing by his desk. "This is Ms. Carla Brewster. She'll represent you."

Carla jumped right in, sticking out her hand for him to shake. "You've obviously got a valid excuse from the court for missing your first appearance." She paused, and he knew exactly what he was going to say. "The problem is, the second you mention it to the DA—"

"They'll use my arrest against me and want me to turn state's evidence against the Heathens. They'll want me to press charges, and they'll make my life miserable because of it," Linc finished. "How much do they know?"

"If they do, they're not saying." She looked between the men. "If you stick to your story, the one you told the doctors at the hospital when you were first admitted, there's not much they can do. That doesn't mean they won't try. They're suspicious."

And they wanted to know who killed Bones and Bruno. Linc was sure of it.

"Just stick to the story, Linc," Sweet reassured him. "Carla will make sure it all works out."

"I'm confident the DA will agree to release you with community service. If you complete that, your record will be expunged. I think that's more than fair." Her voice was as crisp as her white buttoned shirt.

He liked her. He liked no-nonsense people. "That works for me. I'm ready to put this behind me."

"You definitely look ready," Carla said approvingly.

Linc was already dressed for court, his best *I'm a respectable adult* attire, which consisted of a custom-made, dark-gray suit and a white shirt, with a blue-patterned tie he'd been told matched his eyes. And good shoes too, which meant expensive. He'd been guided to buy the entire outfit by Castle, who'd told him that, *"No matter what, a man needs a good suit on his side."*

Linc had to admit he was right, based on the looks he was getting from Sweet and Carla alike.

Twenty minutes later, he and Carla had been escorted to the courthouse door, but Boomer and Tug remained outside. Carla hadn't wanted Linc associated with Havoc, mainly because of what'd happened with the Heathens, and Sweet had agreed.

After Carla checked in with the court officer, she and Linc were escorted into a room outside the courthouse . . . where Castle was already waiting for them inside.

Carla looked between Castle and Linc. "Anything I should know about?"

"I'm just a friend, lending support," Castle said, reaching out a hand for Carla to shake.

Linc was only half-surprised, but it was still a good one. He nodded to Castle as Carla continued. "Who exactly are you? Wait, never mind—deniability is key."

Castle nodded. "My name's Luke Castle. I assume this goes no farther than us. And by that, I mean no one at Havoc can be privy to this information. I know they pay your bills, but this one is being taken care of by me. Tell them you did it pro bono, because you were so taken with what happened to Linc."

"Understood," she told him. "Havoc are good men, Mr. Castle. They make criminal law bearable."

"That, I believe."

She turned to Linc. "And I *am* sorry for what happened to you."

"Thanks." Linc glanced at Castle. "What else is happening here?"

"Closed chambers." He glanced at the door, where the guard was motioning at them through the glass. "I'll take the lead on this, if you don't mind."

"Lead on," Carla said wryly.

"I'd like to know what I'm walking into," Linc told him.

Castle smiled. "The DA wanted you to testify against Heathens. I know Ms. Brewster was going to deny that motion, but the DA was prepared to give you no option beyond that one, or jail time."

Carla frowned. "They're trying to crack down on MC violence. You were a good test case."

"They were going to offer WITSEC," Castle continued.

"Fuck that," Linc muttered.

"And I told the DA that you worked for me and that the arrest was part of your cover." He looked at Linc pointedly, because it absolutely hadn't been, and Matlin hadn't been happy about it. "He relented. The judge is prepared to dismiss. So just keep your mouth closed, be pleasant and polite, and let's get this done."

"It would be great if you came around more often," Carla told him deadpan.

"That could be arranged." Castle was such a goddamned flirt, the way he looked at her. He was also bi, so who knew if they'd get together.

"Before you two start making out, can we get my case dismissed?" Linc asked.

Damn, he was grateful that Castle had showed, because otherwise, he'd have been railroaded by the DA into testifying against the Heathens. They'd heard the rumors about his capture, and even if he'd denied it, they would still have threatened to pin the fire—and the deaths—on him to get his testimony.

And hell, what would he testify about? That the Heathens had kidnapped, drugged, and raped him? That they admitted to killing another man by ripping him apart? That they'd already dug a literal grave for him?

He didn't feel guilt over any Heathens' death, because they were all complicit in one way or another. There wasn't a single redeeming quality about the club, and finding out what they'd done to his brother only strengthened his opinion.

"Heathens as you knew them are destroyed," Castle told the DA.

"They're regrouping," he protested.

"And Linc's testimony has no bearing on that at all. We both know it." Castle stared down the DA. "We're here as a show of good faith, but we both know I could've snapped my fingers and made this whole thing go away. So let's make this as painless as possible, for all of us. You'll agree not to blow Linc's cover—and if it is blown, we'll know exactly who to come after . . . and in return, Linc won't get into any more bar fights. At least ones he needs bail for."

The judge appeared to have already signed off on this. The DA was pissed but had no choice but to agree. And ten minutes later, Linc was released on his own recognizance.

"And what do we tell Havoc about community service?" Carla asked.

"Let's say that the judge felt he'd suffered more than enough, and that he was impressed by his Army record." Castle gave Linc a nod. "Your record's clear."

"Thanks—both of you," Linc told them.

Castle disappeared into the crowd. Linc was used to him doing so, but Carla seemed both impressed and uneasy. "Is he always like that?"

"Pretty much." Linc's phone beeped, and when he glanced down at it, he saw a text from Castle. *Lunch at the diner on 5th. 1PM. Important.*

Linc texted back an affirmative. It would give him plenty of time to go back to Havoc, change, check out more on his missing skip . . . and possibly ask Castle for some help.

Except he had a sinking suspicion that Castle was going to ask him the same thing.

CHAPTER 18

SUSPICIOUS MINDS

Linc went back to the bonds shop to check in, and then he told Tug he was meeting Rush at the diner, which was a couple of blocks away.

It wasn't exactly a lie—Rush had mentioned he'd be at the diner until twelve thirty, and so Linc's exact words to Tug were, "I'm going to try to catch Rush at the diner. Either way, I'm starving."

Tug dropped him there but didn't come inside. "Text me when you're done."

"I can just walk back to the shop . . ."

"Text me," Tug said.

Linc didn't argue, just headed into the diner and went toward the back. This place wasn't a Havoc-owned establishment, but one of the town's most well-loved spots. Havoc was respectful of that fact, but since Linc didn't wear the cut, it was fine for him to stroll in.

Castle had taken a booth in the very back of the place, and he'd taken the side facing outward. It was far enough away from any windows, and Linc figured he'd scoped the place out and picked the spot on purpose.

Linc sank into the seat across from him as Castle was giving the waitress his order. Linc glanced quickly at the menu and ordered a burger and fries.

"Be right back with your drinks," she told them.

Linc nodded at her and then glanced at Castle. "Thanks for the invite."

"I'm assuming you didn't tell anyone who you were meeting."

"If I had, you'd be surrounded by Havoc."

Castle nodded and waited for the waitress to put their drinks down before saying, "Nice suit earlier."

Linc rolled his eyes. "Pat yourself on the back a little harder."

Castle grinned. "And thanks for running interference."

"It's the least I could do. They shouldn't have tried to put you in that position to start with."

"I'm the one who got myself arrested," Linc mumbled, and Castle frowned and looked like he was going to say something, but didn't. "I mean, I know Matlin wasn't happy about it."

"Matlin's no longer your concern. He should've gotten the arrest kicked from the start." Castle didn't bother to hide his irritation.

"I wish you'd let me take care of him."

"You don't need any more trouble, Linc," Castle told him in no uncertain terms. "Understood?"

"Fine. Whatever." Just what he needed—another man telling him what to do. Like he wasn't full up on that shit already.

"I hope this lunch date isn't taking you away from something important."

"I'm going back to work at the bonds shop after this. But you knew that, right?"

Castle sighed. "Sounds serious. Like it's a real job."

"It's keeping me busy. Out of trouble." He wasn't sure which one of them he was trying harder to convince.

"Got your orders, boys." The waitress put their plates in front of them. "Let me know if you need anything else."

They ate in silence for a few moments, until Castle asked, "This is your life now? Catching two-bit criminals for a one-percenter motorcycle gang?"

"Club," Linc replied automatically, forcing himself not to get angry at Castle's words. "And they've got clubs all over here. But thanks for your concern."

"I like looking out for my friends." Castle took a bite of his sandwich.

Linc snagged a fry, dipped it in ketchup, and popped it in his mouth. "I'm good at bond work."

"Of course you are," Castle said seriously. "You'd be good at anything you do."

Linc stared at him. "You mean that?"

"Of course I do. Why are you surprised?" Castle sounded irritated. "I want to see you thrive. You're young. Got a lifetime of opportunities ahead of you. I don't want to see you stuck."

"You think staying in Havoc with Mercy is being stuck?"

"Isn't it?"

"No." For the first time, he'd felt at home. Having Bram here now, along with Rush and Noah, made it that much more complete.

"You'll get restless," Castle pushed. "No matter how happy you are with Mercy, you're going to get bored without the rush of the work you do for us."

"I'll cross that bridge when I come to it." But would that happen too late? Linc considered that over another fry.

Castle seemed to accept that, for the moment. "Let's get to the reason I brought you here. A serious matter has come to my attention, and it involves you indirectly—through Havoc. Your missing skip—Ty—turned up dead . . . in many different pieces." Castle dipped a fry in ketchup. "Dismembered while still alive, for however long that lasted." He ate the fry. "Is Carla seeing anyone from Havoc?"

"Not that I'm aware of." Castle nodded, like he was filing that info away. Linc rolled his eyes. "Can we get off your love life and back on my skip?"

"What do you know about Ty?"

"It didn't make sense," Linc admitted. "Ty was more the public-defender type, so who the hell was paying the high-priced lawyer fee?" Castle leaned back and waited as Linc talked himself through it. "Heathens and PX wouldn't. It's Mexican Cartel. Blanchard intimated that Ty would end up dead . . . and he reps a ton of cartel and Project X guys."

Castle narrowed his eyes. "You met Blanchard?"

"And got Ty's file, but the two aren't mutually exclusive."

"Address on Ty?"

Linc nodded, sent the pictures of the files over to Castle's phone. "Is the cartel working with PX?"

"Depends."

"On what?"

"If you're getting involved."

Linc didn't commit to that. "So the cartel's pulling PX in, and, in turn, they want Heathens. They wouldn't do a drug trade together, because it wouldn't benefit any of them. Which means . . . trafficking."

"Smartest one in the class, as always."

"And Ty?"

"Dead because the DA was trying to use him to build a RICO case against PX and the cartel."

"You knew all about the trafficking, didn't you?" Linc mused.

"We've been hearing rumors, but nothing solid. Actually, I'm thinking you're giving me the first real confirmation, which will get me actual people on this case." Castle looked resigned. "The trafficking of underage kids most definitely is happening, at least through the ports closest to Shades."

Linc's head began to throb. Yeah, this was bad news. The drugs were bad enough, but trafficking brought an even worse element around. "Happy to help."

"Do you want in?"

"Can I tell Havoc any of this?"

"You know the answer to that," Castle said simply.

Which meant he couldn't tell Havoc about the investigation, his part in it . . . or the fact that there was human trafficking happening near Shades Run.

In all the years he'd freelanced for different agencies, recruited right out of the Army, he'd never shared his work with anyone outside of Castle and Matlin. Not with Bram or Rush or Noah. Hell, if Castle even knew he had a brother in the ATF, Linc never knew.

The first time they'd approached him, it'd been for a mob sting in Boston. Apparently, Linc's former CO was friends with Castle, and kept his eye out for men he thought were good chameleons. It was a skill Linc took pride in. Bram was good at it too, so Linc figured it must run in the family. But he'd never wanted to do this full-time. Basically, he still didn't know what he wanted to be when he grew up, and now, as he approached twenty-five, the choices were becoming more cut-and-dried and far more blurry.

The difference between Linc and Bram was that when Linc slid into whatever character he played, he didn't lose himself at all. It didn't fuck with his head—he knew who he was, or he had until the

Heathens had fucked him up good. Still, he was quick on his feet even though he feared that falling for Mercy had made him soft. He hadn't been looking over his shoulder.

But now he had a chance to help Havoc finish the Heathens, once and for all, and get rid of PX at the same time. Because he figured Castle had found a way to bust the drug runners and the traffickers all at once . . . and as Castle talked a little more about the cartel and its interests, Linc got a sick feeling about all of it. Because when Bram had worked to take down a white supremacist gang five years ago, that had been as close to a suicide mission as it got.

Then again, his brother seemed to have a penchant for those.

And pot, meet kettle . . . because now, a new gang threatened Havoc, Shades, and the surrounding towns. The trafficking ring upped the ante to unacceptable levels.

"Trafficking and the mob isn't the typical coupling," Linc observed.

"True. But the cartel and the Aryans go together, and so does cartel and trafficking." Funny how the brotherhood had no problem working for the very non-white cartel when money was involved.

"Fucking cartel in Shades," Linc grumbled.

"Aryans will make the drugs and they'll aid in the trafficking. This way the groups will share the docks and make even more money."

"Aryans don't like to get involved in that shit, so we're missing something," Linc told him. "How am *I* supposed to get involved in this, Castle?"

"You're already involved."

"I don't fit in with the cartel. The mob, yes."

Castle smiled and reassured him. "I'm not having you work to represent the cartel. Your old alias is from the Boston mob family you've already cultivated."

"Johnny O'Connell?" he said doubtfully. O'Connell—or Johnny O.—was a carefully constructed alias, a long-lost cousin who was part of an old Boston mob family who controlled the docks. If anyone wanted in or out without issue, then Johnny O. was the one to see about smooth sailing.

"The cartel's looking to lay cash on someone who can facilitate papers and inspects, and that's you." Castle had a way of making everything look like a walk in the park when it was more like the park was on fire and Linc would be running through it naked with no water in sight.

"And the Heathens? If any of them are there—or even the PX guys—they could make me."

"The cartel doesn't trust the MCs with the final shipment searches. Trust me, Linc—I wouldn't put you face-to-face with anyone who'd make you."

Fuck. "Where are they pulling these kids from?"

"Take your pick of any shelter up and down the east coast."

The docks were about an hour outside Shades and still too close for comfort. Because Bertha's was near the docks and the Havoc kids were used to hanging around there, especially when they snuck out at night.

He thought about the Heathens basement . . . the hands all over him . . . the freshly dug grave . . .

"I didn't realize how much this took from you." Castle's voice tore him from his reverie.

"It didn't . . . not at first. I'm just starting to realize that having the reputation of running isn't always a good thing."

"I'm sorry, Linc."

"I chose the job. That means I'll deal with the consequences. Always have."

Castle reached out and touched his hand. "I've known you a long time. You're hurting."

"Does it matter?"

"To me, it does. I think you're dangerous when you're not working. But if you stay on, you're right—there's going to come a time when your friends—Mercy—have a lot of questions. And you know keeping your circle small is most important. It could be the difference between life and death."

Linc couldn't disagree. He stared out the window. "I need to think about this."

"Don't take too long. The cartel's not."

For most of the day, all Mercy had been able to think about was Linc in that suit . . . holy hell. Mercy had never had a suit fetish but his mind had been changed. It looked expensive. Custom-made. And Mercy needed to find a way to fuck him with it on.

He began making plans for that in earnest once he'd heard how well court had gone. And then, an hour later, when he'd gotten a call from the courthouse about exactly what had gone down, the suit still stayed toward the front of his mind . . . until Tug had called him about Linc's diner lunch date.

After that, Mercy was too busy hunting Bram down on Havoc's compound to think about Linc and suits. He found Bram in the clubhouse, outside of Sweet's office.

"Hey, Sweet's on a call." Bram motioned to the closed door. He'd been heading down the hallway toward the main hangout part of the floor when Mercy barged in.

"Was looking for you. What's your brother up to?" Mercy forced his tone into a pleasant rather than demanding one.

Bram frowned. "Now that the court case is over—"

"I'm not talking about the court case."

"It was dismissed though, right?"

"Yes, it was dismissed," Mercy said. "I'm talking in a more general sense."

Bram still looked confused. "I thought you guys were doing better?"

"We are."

"Like pulling fucking teeth," Bram muttered. "Look, I thought Linc was doing all right. I mean, I thought you worked things out with his sneaking away, and he seems fine at Havoc now . . ."

"It's not that. It's that guy."

Bram looked guarded. "The one from the lake house? He's been coming around still?"

"He was at the courthouse. And Linc's appearance was suddenly in closed court. In chambers."

Bram glanced at the closed door and motioned for Mercy to move farther away from the door. Probably because Sweet had some unnaturally crazy hearing—Mercy had witnessed that firsthand. "What? Carla told you that?"

Mercy shook his head and lowered his voice. "I have eyes inside the court. And if I do . . ."

"Someone else might've seen that," Bram finished. "We need to find out what he's up to, but confronting him isn't the way."

"That's why I came to you. I don't always know how to 'speak Linc,' you know."

Bram snorted. "He'll tell one of us. I think we have to trust that. But my gut tells me . . ." He trailed off, shaking his head like he was trying not to believe what he was thinking.

Mercy was thinking the same damned thing. "Right now, they're meeting for lunch at the diner. Linc lied to Tug and said he was meeting Rush instead."

Bram shook his head. "Doesn't make sense—Linc's allowed to have friends. There's no reason for him not to talk about the guy unless . . . he's not supposed to."

"Which would mean . . . maybe he'd involved with something undercover." And from the way Bram glanced at him, Mercy's suspicions were confirmed. "Does it surprise you?"

"Yes and no. Linc is actually perfect for that line of work. Maybe even better than me. He's more balanced . . . and if it's true, then he was picked early, while he was still in the Army."

"And he said that guy is an old Army friend," Mercy said slowly. "Which means . . . when I thought he ran . . . *fuck*, he could've been on a job?"

Bram shook his head. "Does it matter? Either way you need to believe that he was coming back to you. Because that was his plan, before Heathens got involved."

He nodded, feeling miserable as fuck.

"We'll keep an eye on him," Bram promised. "If Castle's around this much, he's got to be his handler."

"Where was he when Linc went missing?"

"I have no idea, but if I get him alone it's the first question I'm asking. Because I don't like him."

"Makes two of us. Want to roll him and punch him until he talks?" Mercy asked hopefully.

"Yes, but let's drag him to somewhere private."

"Are you two really conspiring to kidnap and beat someone?" Sweet hissed and both men jumped, since he'd snuck up behind them out of nowhere. Then he smirked, like he knew he'd bested them, before warning, "Back off."

"But I don't know this guy—or anything about him," Bram said, like that excused everything else.

Well hell, to Mercy it definitely did, but judging by the look on Sweet's face, he had a different opinion entirely.

"Last I looked, Linc was a free man." Sweet's tone was gruff and his words felt like a punch to Mercy's gut, but it wasn't a lie.

"Linc's too vulnerable. And that guy . . . there's something . . ." Bram crossed his arms and shook his head.

"Have you thought about just asking him?" Sweet suggested.

Bram looked at him like he was crazy. "Fuck no. That's not how we operate. I steal around, find out the truth, and then I'll confront him."

Mercy snorted. Because yeah, that was pretty much his modus operandi.

"I'm going to ask him," Sweet announced.

"No!" Bram yelled, looked at him in horror. "You'll fuck up my whole recon."

Sweet shook his head and muttered something about "crazy-assed bullshit."

"Yeah, and you love my crazy-assed bullshit," Bram retorted, and Sweet smiled and Mercy?

Pretended to gag before interrupting their love-fest to ask, "How does Linc know about Jethro?"

Sweet frowned and Bram shrugged. "No idea. He introduced me to Jethro at the hospital. Jethro told me who he was, so I thought maybe it was more of an open secret than it really is."

"Kept close to the vest. Unless Linc knew through Rush," Sweet said.

But if Linc had been working jobs in any undercover capacity, that would make a lot of the puzzle pieces fit.

Linc would be a good fit in the undercover world. He was calm and balanced . . . or had been, until he'd gotten involved with Mercy.

You dragged him into trouble. Ruin everything you touch.

That's what David's family had told him, when they learned exactly how David died. They knew why, even though the police refused to investigate. Because the police were in bed with the Heathens back home . . . and because David's body had never been found. To this day, he was still listed as MIA, and his parents had been unable to give him a proper burial.

Mercy shook his head. "There's more to it. He and Jethro have known each other a long time. It predates Rush's history with Havoc. Castle's the key to all this shit. He's been hanging around since Linc got hurt."

"Castle's name is on the deed for the lake house and he hasn't cashed any of my rent checks," Bram added. "Which means he and I definitely need to have a long talk."

"Start with Jethro," Sweet instructed. "Because if Linc is working with Castle, he's not going to tell you anything without Linc's approval."

CHAPTER 19

A LITTLE LESS CONVERSATION, A LITTLE MORE ACTION, PLEASE

Linc left Castle at the diner and went out to meet Tug, who brought him back to the bonds shop. Linc didn't mention anything about Ty, not yet, but he was definitely distracted. Tug took pity on him when he started pacing and drove him back to Mercy's house well before five.

Linc couldn't get his mind off what Castle had told him, about the imminent danger . . . about not being able to share it with his friends at Havoc. Now, he slipped into Mercy's house and closed the door quietly. He turned and found himself staring at Mercy . . . who was waiting, leaning against the kitchen counter, arms crossed, but smiling.

A dangerous smile.

"Hey, Mercy."

"Hey, Linc. Heard court went well today."

"Yeah, it did."

Mercy obviously suspected something happened in that courthouse, but if this was going to be his approach, Linc was goddamned fine with it. A win-win, as they said. And, surprisingly, there were no questions, no mentions of court other than, "I'm glad you can put the arrest behind you."

Mainly because of the way Mercy was staring at him, Linc realized he still had his suit on, although he'd taken his jacket off earlier and the tie hung loose around his neck. "Thanks. I'm just going to go, ah, change."

Mercy shook his head. "You look comfortable enough to me. Why don't you hang out here for a while?"

And then Mercy pulled out a wide leather chair from the table and sat, his legs slightly spread, his open palms resting on his muscular thighs.

He knows something. He knows and he's going to torture it out of you. "Okay, yeah, I'll hang. Maybe we could put on a movie."

"I wasn't really thinking about watching a movie. But I did have some thoughts about what else we could do."

"Okay." *You'll be fine as long as he doesn't talk dirty to you . . .*

"Linc? Why don't you come over here and let me suck on those pretty nipples of yours until you're squirming in my lap?" Mercy's suggestion was a casual growl and fuck, how did he know?

"I'm, ah, good here. Thanks." Fuck, his voice hadn't squeaked like that since he'd been twelve.

"Wasn't a suggestion." Mercy patted his thighs and Linc shook his head, even as his legs moved him a few steps closer, registering the inevitable surrender. "After I suck and bite, I might let you come, all over yourself. Or maybe I'll stop you, bend you over this table." His fingers lingered over the wooden table behind him.

Before Linc could eke out another word, he was fully clothed in Mercy's lap, straddling him.

"Good boy," Mercy said approvingly, and only Mercy could get away with calling him that . . . and only in situations like this. He knew Linc's weak spots, and Linc's weakness for him, in bed and otherwise.

But there was something to be said about being so free in bed, and being with someone who let you be that free, because that translated into letting you be free in all other areas of your life and your relationship.

But it was hard, because Mercy could see right through him . . . and right now, Linc didn't want to be seen.

Mercy knew it too, and that made it both better and that much worse. Because what they'd done so far? Fucking tame compared to the way they'd been. And it had been good, still, but this? This was *very* familiar.

"By the way . . . our test results came in," Mercy said as he used Linc's tie to pull him closer. "We're both negative."

Linc's heart thudded. "Good. No more condoms. Unless . . ."

"Unless what?"

"Unless you don't want to be exclusive," Linc whispered.

Mercy's smile became even more wicked. "I'll show you how exclusive we're going to be, baby."

Linc didn't think it was possible for his dick to get any harder . . . but it began to twitch and throb, and he figured he could probably come on the spot if Mercy commanded him to. As if he knew, Mercy smirked, then rucked up Linc's shirts so he could slide his hands underneath to touch Linc's skin, then skimmed his palms along Linc's chest, thumbs brushing his nipples, which were always too fucking sensitive for their own good. "You like that, baby?"

Mercy demanded answers, even though his tone wasn't angry.

"Yes," Linc managed, voice wavering slightly. Mercy took pity on him and rolled Linc's nipples between his thumb and fingertips, causing Linc to arch back and then press into his hands. "Fuck, Mercy . . . that's . . ."

"What you need." Mercy squeezed, then stopped for a quick moment to strip Linc of his shirts, although after he took off Linc's undershirt and discarded it, he put Linc's dress shirt back on him, half buttoned up.

Linc got it then—Mercy was into the goddamned suit, and maybe Linc wasn't in as much trouble as he thought about Castle . . . or maybe he was.

He couldn't stop to consider it because Mercy definitely wasn't stopping. At all. He used the tie to bind Linc's hands behind his back and then, without further hesitation, he leaned in. Pushing the shirt out of the way, he sucked a nipple hard, then bit it with just enough bite to make Linc groan in surrender as the jolt of passion went from his nipple to his groin in a straight goddamned line of lightning.

Mercy murmured, "You just let go, Linc. You make yourself come just from my tongue and then I'll spread you, fuck you . . . make you beg. Just like you like."

Linc knew anything he said would come out a jumble of incoherence. And then he didn't give a shit—Mercy punished his nipples with tongue, teeth and fingers, as Linc was forced, with his cock trapped in his pants, to writhe against Mercy to make himself come. All of this was Linc's kink and Mercy had known it from the start. Coincidence or fate, Linc didn't know and why the hell should he care when it felt this good?

All he cared about was coming. Hard. Stars swam behind his eyes as his entire body let out an exaggerated shudder. He remained pressed to Mercy, until Mercy pulled him off, half carried him to the kitchen table, and began stripping his pants down around his ankles, rubbing his come into his belly, getting it on his own fingers and tracing Linc's ass with it, slicking him.

Then he bent Linc over the table, chest down, before untying his hands from behind his back . . . only to retie them as they stretched out in front of him.

"Spread your legs, baby," Mercy urged, helping him balance, then using his fingers, slicked with Linc's come, to open him up. "Good boy, Linc. Let me hear you whimper. Have you splayed out here, helpless. Doors unlocked. Maybe I should just open it and let everyone see you like this. I'm betting they'll hear you beg and come running to take a turn."

"Mercy . . . Christ . . . please." He didn't even know what he was begging for anymore. He heard the scrape of the chair on the floor and then Mercy's hands were on his ass cheeks, holding him open.

Blowing on his hole.

Linc squirmed—pleasure mixed with humiliation. He tried to hump the table but he couldn't. The friction was minimal and he needed . . . so much more.

Mercy leaned in and licked Linc's hole, a hot drag that made him keen. "You'll do what I say?"

But before he let Linc answer, Mercy buried his face and began to eat his ass, holding him open, sucking, licking, laving a trail of hot fire that threatened to overwhelm him. Linc's legs were shaking, and he couldn't hide his complete and utter pleasure the torture Mercy's tongue was bringing to him. Mercy sucked at his hole, then licked, then fucked him with it, and he was almost to the point of incoherence. He wasn't anything but raw need, exploded nerve endings and pure sensation.

Finally, Mercy pulled back and asked again, "You'll do what I say?"

"Yes," Linc practically sobbed. "Anything, Mercy . . . please, yes . . ."

"Across my lap after this—no questions asked."

"Yes, please—I need . . ."

"Tell me what you need."

"You. Your cock in me. Fucking me. Filling me. Your hand on my ass—all of it." Christ, he couldn't babble fast enough, the relief of the court case being dismissed, coupled with the tension from the Castle meeting, and he needed Mercy to untwist him.

Mercy's fingers and tongue withdrew completely after Linc's verbal compliance, and Linc whimpered from the sudden loss of contact. Cold lube squirted onto his hot skin, a brief respite.

Linc was flat-footed on the ground, chest held against the table, being spread and teased. Then Mercy's cock pressed his hole, and Linc groaned at the intrusion. Even though Mercy had worked him open, it would always burn.

"So goddamned tight, Linc. You're like a vise." Mercy gritted his teeth as he pushed forward. Both were slick with sweat, panting. Mercy bottomed out and Linc swore he could feel the man's gaze staring at the way his cock had to look, buried in Linc. "So hot, baby. You should see how good my cock looks filling your sweet ass."

Linc's only response was a keening wail, because Mercy had pressed forward, hard, hitting his gland.

Mercy held Linc down because he was almost vibrating off the table.

"Mercy, please." Linc was practically clawing the table, splaying his fingers to try to catch the edge and stay put. "Mercy, I'm . . ." The words were barely out when Linc came, his cock spurting between his belly and the table, the friction he'd gotten there leaving him unable to do anything but grind against it like a fucking whore.

Mercy didn't stop hammering inside of him, which stretched his orgasm out, until finally Mercy came and Linc felt him throb inside of him, felt the thick stream of come filling him.

And then Mercy pulled out, pressed his mouth to Linc's hole, and sucked. Linc couldn't fight it, just lay there, boneless. Mercy came back up and laid his body over him, pulled Linc's head so he could reach Linc's mouth. Kissed him, and let Linc taste his own come, which Linc sucked eagerly.

Christ, when had he become such a slut for this man?

Before they took you. And now again . . .

Linc wanted to sob with relief. Even as Mercy eased him off the table and walked him to the couch, made him lie over his lap and brought his hand down on his bare ass, making him count until he came again all over Mercy's legs, the tears shining in his eyes were because Linc knew he could be him again. Maybe not all the time, maybe not even tomorrow . . . but now. Right now.

And that was all that counted.

Mercy practically carried his boy upstairs and held him up in the shower to wash him off. Linc remained half wrapped around him as Mercy soaped them both, murmuring to him.

He dried them and put cream on Linc's reddened ass as Linc lay facedown on the bed, a soft smile on his face.

"You okay, baby?"

"More than," Linc assured him.

Mercy was hard—again—and he wanted to bury himself inside of Linc again. But he wouldn't push it.

CHAPTER 20

DON'T DO ME LIKE THAT

Linc went into the bonds shop the next day and once again avoided talking about Ty. Luckily, the shop was busy, thanks to several bar fights the night before, and that kept his mind off having to think about Ty or Castle's offer. Last night, Mercy had kept him busy as well. Linc could avoid thinking all together.

Tug had to get back to Havoc early for church, so Rush was his ride today. By the time Linc locked up, Rush was out of his car, talking to Harry. Harry was the son of one of Havoc's men, an eighteen-year-old senior who was the ringleader of most of the high school-aged kids on the compound, and he and Rush were laughing.

"Hey, Linc—heard court went well yesterday. I'm glad." Harry gave him a nod as he walked away from Rush.

"Yeah, it did. Thanks." Linc went to his friend. "So the entire compound knows about my court date."

"Did you expect anything less?"

"I guess not." He looked to where Harry's truck was pulling away. "What was that all about?"

Rush smiled. "He just had to share some information with me. He does as much sneaking out as you do."

Linc ignored that. "And he tells you about it?"

"He likes to know he's got a backup, just in case. It's smart, mainly because he brings half the Havoc kids with him."

"Where do they go?"

"The park near Bertha's. It's far enough away from Havoc and it's not heavily policed. Pretty private." Rush shrugged. "They don't do it often and since the lockdown, they haven't gone near the place. But maybe when they sneak out on Friday, you can catch a ride with them."

Linc tensed, but he managed to tell Rush, "Ha ha. Funny."

The smile left Rush's face. "Want to tell me what Castle was doing here yesterday?"

Had Rush spied on him in the diner? Did Tug know? Did Mercy? "He lives in the area, remember?"

"Oh, okay." Rush glanced at him. "And that's it?"

"And that's it."

"C'mon, Linc."

"What? Do you get to question me like Mercy now too? Do you have a report to fill out?" Linc shifted irritably.

"Fuck off, Linc. Why can't you just answer the question?"

"Because I don't have to."

Rush walked around to the driver's side and Linc joined him inside the car. Rush pulled away from the curb before continuing his line of questioning. "Why can't you just tell me? What are you hiding?"

"And here I thought I was all done with court."

Rush didn't say anything for a long while, not until they pulled onto Havoc land. "You were gone, Linc, and I didn't even know. I was wrapped up in a job and Sweet didn't want to worry me and when he did tell me, I figured you were just . . . being you."

"So you're going to track my every move from now on so that never happens again?"

"Fuck you." Rush stopped hard in front of Mercy's house.

Linc went to get out of the car, but Rush locked the doors. Like that would stop him. "More questions, *Sean*?"

Rush turned to face him, his voice hard. "You slept with Castle, didn't you?"

"Today? No."

"So you *did* fuck him. Is that why you got such good grades?"

"Oh fuck you hard, Sean," Linc shot back irritably.

"You barely paid attention, you didn't study, and you were still top of the class."

"I'm a good test-taker."

"Yeah, how exactly were you taking those tests?"

"You're serious?" Linc heard the anger and hurt in his own voice. If Rush had been joking, teasing, that would be cool with him, but he wasn't kidding, and fuck. "What the hell do you think of me?"

"You sleep with a lot of people."

"So that means I do it to get ahead in my life? It was a couple of classes. They didn't get us a pay raise."

Granted, it had brought the FBI's attention to Linc, but that was based on rifle quals and other factors. His test scores in that class had pushed him over the edge but he definitely hadn't fucked Castle to get them. Just the opposite, in fact. And the fact that one of his best friends thought that . . . "Forget it. I thought you knew me."

"I do know you, Linc. When things get hard or scary, you run." Linc just stared at him as Rush continued. "And you ran and got yourself in trouble with Heathens because you couldn't be bothered to confide in me—or anyone."

Rush was angry and frustrated—no more than Linc was—but Linc was too stunned to even speak.

Instead, he unlocked the door and got out, slamming the door behind him. But Rush rolled the window down and called after him, "Right—run the way you always do, Linc."

Linc ignored him as a hot wave of shame and anger covered him, and he kept walking until he was safely inside the house. It was only then that he heard the rev of Rush's car leaving, pealing away from the curb, and he realized he didn't have the luxury of not thinking any longer.

CHAPTER 21

EVERYBODY'S HAD TO FIGHT TO BE FREE

Mercy heard Rush's voice calling to Linc, heard Linc come in and slam the door, but didn't think anything of it . . . not until he came into the kitchen and found Linc had walked out onto the back porch, leaving the door opened behind him.

"Linc, what's going on?" Mercy took in Linc's clenched fists and the fact that his body was practically vibrating with anger, looking into the now-darkening sky.

He heard Linc's breaths, harsh and pulling, and he moved closer. "Linc, come on, talk to me."

Linc shook his head but he turned and faced Mercy with a look of utter despair on his face.

Mercy tried again. "Are you hurt physically?"

Linc shook his head no.

"Do you want me to call someone? Maybe Rush—"

At Rush's name, Linc's eyes hardened and *fuck*, he was upset with Rush? "Linc, I just want you to breathe, baby. You don't have to tell me shit, but just breathe."

Linc let out a breath. Blinked. "It's cold out here."

Mercy guided him inside, sat him on the couch, and made him drink a couple of fingers of bourbon, because the man needed to calm the fuck down.

As he poured the drink, he texted Ryker. *What the hell between these two?*

Bad fight. Rush isn't talking, but he's upset as fuck.

After Linc downed the drink, Mercy gave him a second one, which Linc nursed.

Mercy sat across from him. "So, you and Rush had a fight."

"Yeah."

"It's never easy when it's a best friend. Sweet and I . . . well, we've had our share of knock-down, drag-outs over the years. We've come to blows. We've gone weeks without talking. We tend to hurt those we love the most, and it's usually because we're scared."

Linc downed the rest of the second drink. "You done, Dr. Phil?"

Mercy couldn't help it—he laughed. That made Linc snort and then he sat back and smiled.

"It can be fixed," Mercy assured him.

"Maybe. But I can't change people's perceptions of me. Not someone I trust."

"He's worried."

"Are you?"

"Yes."

"You think I run when the going gets tough?"

"I think you like your freedom. I think you're hiding something that could explain a lot. But I think loving you means trusting you, so that's what I'm doing."

Linc stood and walked over to where Mercy sat, climbed into his lap, and sank against him. "Thank you, Mercy."

Mercy's arms went around him. "Anytime, baby."

"I wasn't running from you. I wasn't."

"I believe you. I should've known it then."

Linc hugged him hard. Mercy felt the sobs, silent as they were, and he just murmured that everything would be fine until Linc calmed.

By that point, Linc was practically asleep. Mercy carried him to the couch and laid him down, covered him with a blanket, and put his phone within reach. Left him a text saying he was going out on patrol and to call when he woke up.

Fuck, he hated leaving Linc, but hopefully he'd sleep for the next few hours and then Mercy would be done with patrols. He was just going out with Tug and Boomer to a new bar on the strip on the very edge of town that was supposedly being shaken down by Pagans.

"Pagans are trying to make it their place in Shades," Boomer had explained. "With the Heathens trying to regroup, I'd be surprised if they weren't trying for a total takeover."

As friendly as Pagans and Heathens were, Mercy could believe it to be true. For the twenty-minute ride, he let the road own him, soothe him, and rile him up, all at once. It was similar to what Linc did to him—and for him, he realized.

Their attraction had been immediate and intense. Unmistakable. It was no coincidence that Linc was the first person he'd ever met (and he'd met a lot of people along the way) that Mercy was both attracted to and jealous of at the same time . . . because Linc was a free bird, and watching him simply enjoy himself had been a thing of goddamned beauty.

Linc was also the polar opposite of Mercy's first love, David, because David and Mercy'd both had to hide who they were, at least for a while. Linc didn't give a shit who knew he was bi. Hadn't cared when Mercy began making out with him in the middle of Bertha's, and later at the Havoc clubhouse.

Later that night, Mercy had fucked him in one of the back rooms, over and over, and they'd ended up passing out together.

He hadn't wanted to let Linc go. And considering the first time he'd met Linc was after bailing him out of jail post bar fight, as a favor to Rush and Ryker, that was saying something. He never mixed business with pleasure. Not until that night and it was no exaggeration to say that his life had never been the same since.

Honestly, he'd never expected to have kept his secret forever, but his worst nightmare was knowing that an innocent person had gotten hurt because of him and his connection to the Heathens.

Again.

And it had been a nightmare.

That's why he was back enforcing. No more fucking nightmares would be created on his watch.

As they approached, they saw Pagans bikes parked outside. There were sounds of glass breaking inside.

Tug smiled. "Going to be fun to kick their asses tonight."

Mercy couldn't agree more.

Linc woke to the sound of his text messages dinging. He grabbed the phone and noted he'd been asleep for maybe three hours or so . . . and that the phone had saved him, because he'd been on the brink of a nightmare. Even now, he shuddered as though the Heathens had just been touching him as he sat up and saw Mercy's texts.

He was immediately torn between pleased and concerned . . . because Mercy had promised to tell him shit, and his texts admitted, *Found some trouble. At the clubhouse getting a couple of stitches. No big deal. Be home soon.*

Right. Rather than stay here and jump out of his own fucking skin with worry, Linc took his truck, rather than his bike—so he could drive Mercy home—and made the trip down the hill. He found Misha there with Sweet and Mercy, who had a good-sized bandage on his arm.

"It's just a small nick from a knife," Mercy told him before he could say anything.

"Twenty stitches. Big knife," Misha corrected.

"Traitor," Mercy muttered.

"Truth teller," Misha corrected lightly, then told Linc, "He needs to stay here and finish this IV. No riding for two days. And he needs to take these three times a day."

"Am I a child who can't follow directions?" Mercy asked.

"Yes," Misha and Linc told him at the same time.

Misha continued, "I'll be back to look at the bandage before you leave, and I'll stop by tomorrow. But if it keeps bleeding, or bleeds more heavily, or if he's running a fever—"

"I've got your number," Linc assured her.

"I'll be back in twenty."

"How's Tug?" Linc asked Mercy when Misha left.

"He's already stitched up. His wrist is sprained."

"And Boomer?"

"He's been happier, but ultimately he'll be fine."

"Pagans?"

"Yes, for the most part. They were with some PX guys too, trying to shake down that new bar." Mercy looked like he didn't want to say anything further but reluctantly added, "Rumors are that they're working with a cartel. I can't confirm that, but Project X was hanging out too close to Shades."

"Selling?"

"I don't know," Mercy admitted. "Two nights ago, Vann caught them . . . and you don't have twenty skinheads in a public park at midnight having a bible reading."

"Actually—"

"You know what I'm saying, smart-ass. But we sent a message. Vann followed them to the border and waited to make sure they didn't double back. He also planted a tracker on them. We called him to the bar tonight and he stayed to help the owner clean up before he called the police. He's on his way here now."

Linc had to let Castle know this. If he didn't get involved . . . if he didn't tell Mercy and Sweet that they needed to watch Havoc's kids, it would be on his conscience, more than it already was.

Fuck. He texted Castle quickly, saying, *I'll take the job.*

Castle texted back immediately. *Details to follow shortly.*

He thought about mentioning what Rush told him, about how the Havoc kids planned to sneak out this Friday night, but held off until he could tell Castle in person.

When he looked up, Mercy was staring at him. "Everything all right?"

"It's going to be."

Mercy smiled. "Take me home, Linc."

CHAPTER 22

REST YOUR WEARY HEAD
AND LET YOUR HEART DECIDE

When they got home, Linc could see that Mercy was tired. He'd taken only half a painkiller but the adrenaline rush was waning. So Linc got him up to bed, and almost as soon as Mercy was out, Linc was too.

The Heathens were there—Bones and his friends—but instead of grabbing him, they grabbed Mercy and pulled him away, out of Linc's grasp. Mercy was reaching for him, but the Heathens were stronger . . .

He heard screams and realized they were his. But still, Linc was caught halfway between dreaming and waking, and Mercy was reaching out his hands to him and Linc couldn't leave him behind . . . wouldn't . . .

"Linc, baby, come on. You're safe."

It took several long moments to process Mercy's voice—and the fact that Mercy was there with him, holding him. "They didn't take you," he murmured, and Mercy frowned. A shudder went through Linc's body and he realized he was soaked with sweat.

"You're safe," Mercy repeated firmly. "Come on—let's get you cleaned up."

Linc wanted to wash the entire dream away, so he let Mercy help him up and into the shower. Mercy basically held him up, washed him down, and dried him before sitting him down in a chair so he could change the sweaty bedding.

Finally, Linc was settled back in bed with water. Mercy pulled him close and Linc traced the tats on his biceps and chest like he was memorizing them. "Sorry."

"Don't you dare apologize for that," Mercy told him fiercely. "If you have to have them, I want to be here to help you."

Linc assumed that seeing Mercy hurt, knowing he was patrolling and that a rival gang had stabbed him, was what made the nightmare tonight particularly intense. But dammit . . . "You and I . . . we're getting closer . . . I thought it would get better."

Mercy shook his head. "It doesn't work like that. We are getting closer, baby. But that's going to bring things to the surface more strongly. That's why your nightmares have been getting worse, not better."

"Shit. So it's never going to stop?"

"Not until we talk about it. We *need* to talk about what happened to you."

"Because we've been pretending things are fine?"

"Because you've been trying to prove you're fine." Mercy's tone cut through any bullshit Linc might throw at him. "You're not, and you won't be. Not until you talk about what happened to you."

"To a shrink?"

"If you want. I'd prefer you tell it to me," Mercy admitted and Linc frowned. "I'm the one you're trying to protect, to hide things from. And that's not doing you any favors . . . because I know."

"If you already know, then . . ."

"It's not the same as you talking about it, Linc—you know it. You're coming back, yes, but your PTSD episodes are going to get worse with every job you do if you can't try to put what happened in your rearview."

"Pretend it never happened."

"That's not possible. But you have to accept that it did and refuse to let it rule your future."

Linc wrapped his arms around himself. "Are you over what happened to you? Because Rush told me that, in all the time you've been with Havoc, you've never committed to anyone."

"He's right."

"What did your old MC do to you, Mercy? Is it something you can't get over?"

"Heathens took someone I loved. The last person I committed to was someone I also claimed, for his own protection, because he was with me. It was when I was seventeen. Turns out he needed protection from my own MC and my family, which were one and the same."

"Because it was a guy."

Mercy nodded. "They tried to force me to be something—someone—I'm not. In the end, I took the easy way out and I ran."

"That's not the easy way out. That's called survival. Live to fight another day, and you did that. You've been fighting them ever since. You're aligned with good people."

Mercy nodded. "I know that now. It took a long time. I talked about it with Sweet. I told him everything. Then I changed my name. Picked it as a nice *fuck you* to my family. I figured the name Mercy fit in a couple of different ways." He shrugged. "They always said I didn't fit with them. Didn't look like them. I heard it my entire life. Bad enough to be considered an outsider in society when you're with your family, but when you're not good enough for them, either, it can really fuck you up. But I've never been ashamed of what I am or of who I am." He paused. "Now it's your turn to talk to me."

"How's this going to help anything?" Linc's voice was a whispering plea.

"Because you need to move it out of your head and out here." Mercy widened his arms. "Share that burden."

"Because you do that so well."

Mercy sighed. "Cards on the table, for both of us."

"I already know your cards, Mercy, and you know mine, so how's this going to help?"

"It will, Linc. Because I'm not the one having screaming nightmares." Mercy's tone was kind despite his brutal honesty. "Tell me. Now. Tell me your demons."

Of course Mercy would order him, because it would make it easier for him to comply. "Please, Mercy . . ."

"I know you don't want to tell me. But until you say it—out loud—you're not going to heal. And trust me, I know what you're going to tell me, baby. I know, because I saw it happen when I was a Heathen."

Linc's breath caught in his throat as Mercy continued. "Once I knew they had you, I couldn't wait for anyone else's plan. Bram was going to trade himself for you, and he would've. But it was my turn to step up and do something that I should've done years ago. So tell me, dammit. Purge yourself."

Linc swallowed hard. "Bones liked to stay close to me. He's the one I remember most clearly. He's the one who told me about David. What they did to him." He didn't want to do this, talk about it, but fuck, he saw it in his dreams every damned night. "He said it was what Heathens did to their own who were traitors. And they knew you were gay and they tried to fix you, but it didn't work. And so they were going to show you what they'd do to anyone you touched—that was the best way to torture you rather than just kill you outright."

Linc took a long drink from the water bottle next to the bed. He held it, stared at it, even as he felt Mercy's eyes on him in the dark, and then he continued, his voice halting. "They tied David's arms and legs to two different motorcycles and they . . ." He pressed his fist to his forehead. "Dammit—don't make me say it."

"Is knowing what happened to David . . . thinking what they'd do to you . . . is that what has you waking up screaming at night?"

Linc met his eyes. "Yes. But I don't want to . . . I can't tell you . . ."

"I know exactly what they did to him."

Linc looked up at him in surprise. "How?"

"It's not a secret what Heathens do to their own. Not to another Heathen, anyway, although that's well hidden. It's a special punishment, meted out for traitors."

"It's what they would've done to Bram if they'd gotten their hands on him again." Linc's voice was barely there.

"Yes."

"Did Bram know?"

Mercy shook his head. "He wouldn't have—not until it happened. It's something full members know."

"And David—he wasn't a member?"

"No. But since I opened my big mouth and claimed him . . ." He shook his head at the memory. "I never thought they'd do that to him. And I shouldn't have but . . ."

"So that's why you never claimed anyone since him."

"But I did," Mercy reminded him. "I made you mine since the first time my dick was inside you—make no mistake about it. But claiming you out loud, to the world . . . I was afraid it would make you a target."

Linc stilled. "You were trying to protect me."

"I should've known better." Mercy shook his head. "Maybe if you'd had the background on me . . . if I'd told you about the danger . . ."

"I'd have stayed. It wouldn't have changed anything for me. You can't torture yourself like that."

"Then you need to stop torturing yourself too."

Linc gave a small smile. "Just tell me one thing—did you . . ."

"See it done?" Mercy nodded slowly. "It's burned into my memory. But you? Fuck—for the first time, you made me forget it."

"And now I'm just going to remind you of it."

"You remind me that I still have a heart that works. That's all."

"Did they really make you watch what happened to David?"

"They chained me so I couldn't get away. I could've closed my eyes but I wouldn't let David suffer alone," Mercy admitted. "No more of these nightmares for you, baby. It's over and they can't hurt you anymore. I want you free from that. I know it's not that simple but . . ."

Linc wound his arms around him, buried his face against Mercy's neck. "I want it to be."

Mercy's voice was gentle. "What did my brother do to you?"

"Nothing you need to know about. It's not going to do either of us any good."

"I saw your records." Mercy's voice was hoarse.

"And you're seeing me now," Linc shot back. "Look at me—flesh and blood, standing in front of you, naked. Needing you to touch me."

"You can't just push it down."

"Maybe you can't, but that's you. I'm working through it, trying not to hurt myself anymore in the process." Linc paused. "He touched me, okay? He and his friends . . . they used me."

Mercy's expression was tight, pain and anger mixed. "It's usually the men who hate themselves the most who do it. They're angry at their urges. Angry they can't be themselves. I know Bones fooled around with boys when we were growing up, but he always threatened them so they wouldn't talk. He made it more of a dominance thing."

For Linc, the forced sex had been the easy part. The constant, tortured wondering of what would happen next was the hardest to bear.

Linc shook his head. "I didn't ask for any of this, Mercy. But I realize that you didn't either. The only reason I'm telling you this is that I know who killed David. And I know where David's buried."

Mercy looked stunned. Ruined. "How? Why?"

Linc swallowed hard. "Because Bones told me exactly where he was going to bury me. And what he was going to do to me, step by step. And then they took me to see David's grave. They showed me the one they dug for me. They were going to tape the whole thing to show you."

Mercy's arms were around him. "But they didn't. I stopped them. Bones is dead. You're okay. You survived. So goddamned tough, Linc. I think you saved yourself—because they thought you'd crack right away and when you didn't . . ."

"I just kept thinking about you. Bram too. Knew you'd come for me—both of you." He stared at Mercy.

Mercy's mouth opened and when he finally took a breath, it was long and stuttered, sounded like he was sucking air through a straw.

"I never wanted to tell you what happened to David," Linc told him. "It's something I wanted to lock up inside of me."

"Why?"

"To protect you."

Mercy hung his head. "You're stronger than I ever was."

"I think we're pretty equal. And I think we both have enough scars that we don't need to make each other into a whipping boy because of it. But you should be able to give David a proper burial. Let me go with Bram. He can call it in officially. Make it look like it was stumbled on."

"No," Mercy said. "I want them to know Havoc found it."

"Then they'll know I told you."

"Trust me—I'll let the Heathens know."

"Will you do me one more favor?" Linc asked. "I know it's hard because you want to protect me . . . but you can't keep me in a bubble."

Mercy nodded. "I know that. But for now, you still need guys with you when you go anywhere. It's a dangerous time. But . . . that doesn't mean you have to stay on Havoc. That's what the other night was about. Okay?"

Linc nodded. "I just needed to hear you say it. Just like you needed me to."

"Finally, he understands."

Linc rolled his eyes and then leaned in to kiss him. And the kiss went immediately to nuclear. Linc couldn't remember feeling lighter than he did right now.

Mercy pulled back and murmured against his cheek. "You can do anything, Linc. You're strong. I never wanted you to feel helpless. I just want to stop your pain. All of it."

Linc stroked his cheek. "If only."

CHAPTER 23

IT'S SO EASY, WHEN YOU KNOW THE RULES

The kiss had riled Mercy up. There was no way either of them was going to be able to sleep now, not until they'd slaked this constant electric current that ran between them.

He'd pulled Linc's mouth onto his again, wanting to wash away the nightmare, needing to fix this boy who'd shown more goddamned faith in him than Mercy deserved.

And even though Linc was stripping, pressing against him, Mercy knew that he was still feeling vulnerable . . . especially after all they'd discussed tonight. "You want to fuck me, Linc? Because you can."

Linc frowned. "Mercy, I . . ."

"Whatever you need, baby. However you need it." And then Mercy moved away and rifled through the drawer next to the bed, pulling out a pair of handcuffs. He stripped his sweats off and put himself close to the headboard, half lying down and half propped onto pillows, and then he handed Linc the cuffs.

"Use them," Mercy told him, because tonight, he had a feeling it was the only way Linc could tolerate what he needed.

And he *needed*. Mercy could tell from the strain in his eyes, the clench of his jaw. He would resist all of it, and Mercy knew he wouldn't be able to keep himself from touching.

"How do you always know?" Linc asked.

"Because I love knowing things about you."

Mercy did the first cuff himself, hooking it around the headboard. And then he held out the second one to Linc, who finally, reluctantly took it and circled the cold metal around Mercy's other wrist.

Then Linc sat back and studied Mercy for a long moment . . . before a slow, small smirk broke through his tired expression. "At my mercy."

Mercy felt lazy and vulnerable all at once. "Does that work for you?"

"Strangely enough, it does." Linc traced his fingertips along Mercy's pecs, abs before moving them over Mercy's nipples lightly.

Mercy sucked in a harsh breath. "Fucking tease."

Linc straddled Mercy, bent his head to bite Mercy's nipples, hard enough for Mercy to groan in frustration, and then Linc was sucking and biting, riding along Mercy's hard cock. "Definitely."

Linc felt high. Drunk. In control and yet so goddamned out of control all at the same time.

"Ride me, Linc. Lower your tight ass onto my big fat cock and take me all the way in, until I fill you."

"Fuck, Mercy." Linc's face flushed.

"I thought you liked following orders in bed." Mercy looked around. "We seem to be in bed so . . ."

Linc pushed back and ran his hand up the length of Mercy's cock before bending down to suck at the pre-come. Mercy jerked forward and Linc opened his mouth to take whatever Mercy had to give him. Even without holding him in place, Mercy had a hold on him, and Linc stayed put, letting Mercy face-fuck him.

Finally, Mercy pulled back. "Give me your cock, Linc. In my mouth, now."

Linc pushed his sweats down and straddled Mercy's face. Mercy took him in, swallowed him, and it was Linc's turn to fuck his face—hard, watching Mercy's eyes water. But Mercy didn't protest, just hummed around Linc's cock, and Linc found himself fisting one hand into Mercy's hair while shooting hard down his throat. Some of Linc's come dripped from Mercy's mouth, and Linc pushed back and leaned in to lick the trail of come before kissing Mercy, tasting himself.

Just when he thought Mercy couldn't make things any hotter, he went and surprised Linc.

"Want me to feed you your own come, baby? I'll do that next time—all of it," Mercy breathed against his cheek. "Give me your nipples now."

Linc obeyed, because even handcuffed, Mercy had total control over him. And Linc wasn't complaining, not one goddamned bit. He let Mercy suck his nipples until he was struggling not to come ... and he forced himself to ease back. Because he needed to be inside Mercy tonight.

This would be a first, not because Mercy had ever resisted it, but because Linc had never needed it like this. He moved down Mercy's body, sucking red marks on his chest and abs and thighs, licking the thick vein that ran on the underside of his heavy cock—he took in Mercy's groans like a personal victory.

Then he spread Mercy's thighs, pushing his legs up and back so he could have full access to him. First, he licked Mercy's balls, sucked them into his mouth one at a time, then licked the sensitive strip of skin behind them, until Mercy was panting. Begging.

Everything about the Mercy he'd known pre-capture had been easy, and Linc wondered if that had been a lie, or if his change in demeanor had been because of Linc ... because he now had someone to protect. Tonight's discussion had confirmed that.

But now, the Mercy on the bed in front of him? This was shades of the old Mercy, because when Linc buried his face in Mercy's ass and began to lick and lave at his hole to get him ready, Mercy had no problem lying open, bared to him and taking all the pleasure Linc had to give him. It was a joy to see.

"Linc, baby, come on up here and fuck me."

And Linc smiled, used lube and his fingers to open Mercy up more. Finally, he knelt between Mercy's legs and pressed his cock inside of the man who welcomed it. "I don't want to hurt you."

"You won't. Come on, faster," Mercy ordered, but Linc ignored him and took his time, at least until he'd breached Mercy enough to push past the tight ring of muscle. And then he didn't hold back, sliding deeply into Mercy, hitting his prostate and watching Mercy come apart, over and over under him. Until Linc couldn't hold out any longer and his cock throbbed and pulsed and he shot hard inside of Mercy, even as Mercy came in thick, hot ropes between their bodies.

"Missed you," Linc murmured as he collapsed onto Mercy's chest, hoping it made sense to him.

"Sentimental boy," Mercy murmured back. "I was always here . . . waiting for you."

CHAPTER 24

HEART OF GOLD

The next morning, Mercy left early with Sweet and Bram in order to meet up with Vipers to discuss their suspicions about Project X. Linc was glad Mercy didn't have him go along, because he wasn't sure if he'd be able to hold out explaining what he knew . . . and it was only fair that Mercy find out from him first, when they were alone. It was time to tell Mercy about Castle . . . because spilling some secrets last night convinced him to spill the last one he was holding.

To that end, he texted Mercy late morning. *Hey, when you get home, can we talk about something? Wake me if you need to.*

He didn't get a response, but he knew Mercy was traveling on his bike so he wasn't worried. Actually, relief washed over him, because even though he hadn't told Mercy everything yet, it was a matter of hours before he could let his secret out. Castle be damned.

Later that afternoon, Linc was finishing up at the bonds shop when Vann came in. "Let me guess—you're my babysitter for the day."

Vann pretended to look hurt. "Can't a guy just stop by to say hello?"

Linc laughed. "At least Mercy doesn't have Shaman on the roof anymore. Right?"

"Sure, right. Whatever you say," Vann told him unconvincingly.

"Christ. Shaman, time to go home," he yelled up toward the ceiling vent.

Shaman's voice filtered in through the same vent. "You guys going out? I could use a drink."

Vann shrugged. "Works for me."

They ended up at Bertha's, because why not? Vann and Shaman decided to take Shaman's truck and Boomer and Tug would meet them there, since they were still out patrolling that night.

"Won't you get in trouble with Mercy for taking me out?" Linc asked.

"Can't get in touch with him or Sweet—they're out of pocket when they meet with Vipers. And I'm not ringing alarm bells to ask if you can go get a drink," Vann told him. "I thought things were better with you guys."

"They are."

"How much better?" Vann asked, brows raised.

"I'm not giving you details about my sex life."

Vann smiled. "You just did."

Shaman laughed and steered the truck into Bertha's lot. It was a quiet Wednesday night, and it was still early, with dark just settling in. Linc stuck with beer, not tequila, because he needed to have his wits about him to talk to Mercy later.

So when his phone started buzzing about an hour later, he picked it up expecting it to be Mercy, but was surprised to hear Rush's voice on the line.

"Linc, listen, I need your help."

His friend sounded semi-frantic. "What's wrong? Where are you?"

"I'm fine—but I'm nowhere near Havoc. Listen—remember when I told you about Harry and how he sneaks out sometimes?" Linc's gut tightened as he listened. "Harry called—his truck broke down in the park."

"I thought they weren't sneaking out because of the lockdown."

"Yeah, well, me too. In light of what happened last night—well, he hadn't heard about it because Sweet wanted to keep it quiet. But Harry said there's shit happening at the docks and he needs to get him and his friends out of there."

"Text me his number—and then tell him I'm on the way. Tell them to stay quiet and not invite trouble."

"Got it. Be careful, Linc."

"What's wrong?" Vann asked.

"We've got to get to the park . . . but we've got to do it quietly."
Linc explained what Rush told him, and Vann and Shaman got it
immediately. "Listen, you guys need to drop me off and let me go into
the park and lead them out. If we go in with the truck, we'll attract
too much attention and it'll be a goddamned war, with the kids in the
middle."

"I'm going in with you," Vann told him and Linc didn't argue.
They got into Shaman's truck and made the ten-minute ride, during
which Linc called Jethro. "Where are you?" he asked when Jethro
picked up on the second ring.

"You miss me, babe?"

"Not the time for flirting, Jethro—where are you?"

"What's wrong?"

"I need you to head to the park by the docks. Havoc kids are
there—maybe some Hangmen ones too." Linc paused. "There've been
reports of trafficking happening at the dock."

"Shit."

"Mercy and Sweet are two hours out—that's the only reason I'm
not telling them. I'm almost there—Vann and I are going in on foot to
get them out. Shaman's waiting to pick us up. But we can't afford ugly
near those kids."

"We're on it. Five minutes out," Jethro assured him.

"Sounds like the stars are aligning," Vann said quietly. Linc saw
him check his weapons. "You carrying?"

Linc wasn't sure he should admit that he always was, but he
nodded. Vann didn't seem surprised at all.

They raced down the highway, Linc's heart slamming out of his
chest.

"Boomer and Tug are half an hour out," Vann confirmed before
shoving his phone into his pocket. "They'll meet us at Bertha's, if we
don't need them before."

Shaman dropped them off at the edge of the woods at the back
of the park, and Linc and Vann threaded their way through the woods.
They didn't use any lights save for what was already illuminated
by the few streetlights surrounding the park, and it reminded Linc of
his Army days. Vann was quiet, driven, and Linc could easily see the
soldier in him as he moved.

They found the Havoc teenagers in the middle of the park, hiding where the foliage was thickest. Linc texted Harry that he saw them, that it was safe to show himself, and Harry did.

It was obvious they'd been partying—because they'd taken their party with them, more so to hide the evidence from whoever was watching them at the docks and not to continue partying. They were definitely muted, and although Harry maintained control—over himself and the small group with him—the tension came off him in waves.

Vann's growling stares weren't helping.

"You did great," Linc assured him. "You stayed out of sight of the dock. If you'd taken the truck, they'd have followed you. I'll tell your dad how you held it together and took charge."

Harry gave him a grateful smile, and then Linc and Vann led the crew back through the woods and into Shaman's waiting car. As they moved, they all heard commotion coming from over by the docks, starting with the roar of motorcycles and then continuing with shouts. Linc ignored the cold shudder that went down his spine and kept himself—and the kids—moving.

Once they were in Shaman's truck, he pulled away toward Bertha's, with Vann checking their six. "Patrols," he said quietly.

Yeah, the men at the docks definitely had noticed the teens. They were being tailed, but not closely, by some PX bikers. Shaman kept his cool and a fast pace, and although it seemed like hours, it was only five minutes before they pulled into Bertha's big lot.

The PX went past the lot. There was no way they were coming in here. There was also no way these kids could drive home without a show of force.

Linc brought them into the back room and got them each a beer, followed by sodas, and tried to think of the best way to get them into the least amount of trouble. But hell, it was pretty impossible. They'd have to take their lumps, and most of them seemed resigned to it.

After maybe twenty minutes, Linc left them in the back room with Monster standing outside the door, and went to the main part of the bar, where Vann waited.

Jethro had come in and was talking with Boomer. He had scraped knuckles, a torn shirt, and some blood on his face that he quickly wiped off when he saw Linc.

"Hope the other guy looks worse," Vann commented.

Jethro flipped him off. "They all do. We're going to make another sweep and then Casey wants us to escort you guys back home and come back in the morning."

"You've got some Hangmen kids in the back," Linc told him. "A brother and sister."

Jethro nodded. "I'll have a couple of guys bring them back to Hangmen tonight."

When he left, Vann slid over to Linc. "You know what I'm going to ask you." And yeah, Linc did. "How do you know so much about what's happening at the docks?"

"I just do."

"Because of that guy who keeps hanging around."

"Vann—"

"Mercy needs to know this, Linc. We all do."

"I know. I just don't want these kids to get in trouble for doing what kids do."

Vann nodded. "I hear that, but they know about Heathens. They know they shouldn't be out around here—or anywhere right now, so when this is over, they'll get their asses kicked by their parents."

Linc was grateful that Vann didn't point out that he was projecting his feeling onto the kids. Instead, he nodded and Vann said, "Check in with Mercy—I'll call Sweet."

Linc dialed Mercy and this time, he picked up, saying, "Hey, we're just grabbing something to eat. You checking up on me?"

In spite of everything, Linc smiled at the easy tone of Mercy's question. "Listen, we had an issue." There was a pause and he heard Sweet's voice in the background. "I guess you're hearing about it too. Vann was calling Sweet."

"Are you okay, Linc?"

"I'm fine. The kids are fine. We're heading back to Havoc in a few—with an entourage. Hangmen are towing Harry's truck back to their garage and Jethro's monitoring the docks. No trouble—PX dispersed easily."

Mercy was uncharacteristically quiet. "We're heading back now. It'll be a couple of hours. We'll talk then."

Linc barely got "Okay" out before Mercy cut the line. And then they were ushering the kids into both Shaman and Tug's trucks, and Linc and Vann split up. Casey sent Hangmen to follow them halfway back to Havoc—and Jethro ended up following them the entire way back—and they made the rest of the trip without incident.

Linc wasn't sure what went down on the docks—not completely, but he figured Jethro would fill him in. If not, he'd hear it from Castle.

Once the kids were safely back in their houses, Shaman dropped Linc off at Mercy's. Within fifteen minutes, Linc heard the roar of bikes outside and saw that both Vann and Jethro were coming toward him.

He was grateful not to have to wait alone.

"You all right?" Vann asked as he brushed past him and went into the kitchen.

"I'm fine," Linc said automatically as Jethro followed Vann in, carrying a pizza, and they ended up sitting at the kitchen table eating in comfortable silence. "Harry and his friends are all home, safe and sound."

"Was a close call," Vann observed. "Too fucking close."

Linc glanced at Jethro. "Heathens and PX are teaming up, aren't they?"

Jethro sat back. "You really want to ask about the cartel, don't you?"

Linc sighed. "I know it was Project X. I didn't know if they were alone."

"A few Heathens. No Pagans," Jethro confirmed. "No signs of the cartel either . . . but we both know that doesn't mean shit."

"Is that why you freaked out?" Vann asked. "You think the cartel's after Havoc?"

"Not necessarily after Havoc . . . but they're involved in trafficking. They're teaming up with PX," Linc admitted. Of course Jethro didn't look surprised at the admission, and even though Vann didn't really either, it was obvious that it was the first time he was hearing this information. "Mercy mentioned that there was trouble with PX and the cartel being too close to Havoc . . ."

"But Sweet and Mercy don't know about the trafficking," Jethro broke in.

"Not yet. They will," Linc said.

"Good. Too many secrets don't help," Vann told him.

Jethro's phone rang. "Gotta take this." He walked outside, onto the porch, shutting the door behind him.

"You were good tonight, Linc. Really goddamned good." Vann's tone was serious.

"Are you surprised?"

"Not at all. I'm happy to see your PTSD can lift for emergencies. Just a warning—sometimes, after things go well, it kicks into overdrive. The bitch that keeps on giving when you least expect it."

"Sounds like you've got firsthand experience."

"Doesn't everyone who served have it, in one form or another?" Vann shrugged.

"Mine's not from serving. I mean . . ."

"I know," Vann said with a small smile, and for some reason, that broke a little something inside of Linc. He took a deep breath to stave off what felt like a rising panic attack.

Vann was next to him in seconds, leading him to the couch and sitting next to him. "What's happening here, Linc? Try to breathe, kid."

Kid. He snorted and that actually helped stave off the descent into complete panic. "Sorry."

"Nothing to be sorry about."

"It's just . . . I'm fucking trapped, Vann. I get that something bad happened . . . but it's going to define me for fucking ever." To his horror, Linc felt the tears rise. Vann's arm went around him. "I already talked to Mercy about this and I thought that would make it all better. It helped, but fuck, this feels never-ending."

"Do you know why I'm a rogue member of Havoc?" Vann asked.

"No. I figured you just like the freedom, which you know I understand."

"The only one who knows is Sweet, and that's only because he had to know to approve my status. I'm not up for telling you what happened to me . . . but let's say that I understand what it's like to be captured and held, okay?"

Linc stared into Vann's dark eyes and saw how haunted they appeared. No wonder Vann understood him so well. He'd been in Linc's position. "You had to run to heal."

"I ran because I didn't have anyone. Havoc didn't know me well enough. I told Sweet because he needed an explanation. But you have someone. A lot of someones. It's going to take time, Linc. It'll never be the same . . . but that's okay too."

"Vann . . . you're not . . . like Jethro, are you?"

"He's not," Jethro broke in before Vann could, although the look on Vann's face told him that Vann wasn't a fed at all. Linc hadn't heard him come in but Vann must've. "He's former military and all Havoc."

"Just the way I like it," Vann added.

"What do you do for money as a rogue member?" Linc asked.

"Odd jobs."

Linc didn't bother asking what those might be—he could use his imagination. "Is everything okay?"

"Sweet and Mercy are almost here. I'll hang around to talk to them," Jethro said.

"I'm going to talk to Mercy . . . about everything," he said. Vann got up and went into the kitchen and Linc whispered to Jethro, "Mercy's going to be so fucking pissed at me. How can I make this work?"

"It's part of the reason I'm single," Jethro answered honestly. He sat next to Linc now and circled an arm around him protectively. There was nothing sexual about his touch. "Does Castle know what you're about to do?"

"No. And I don't give a fuck."

"So you're prepared to give that up?"

"I guess I am. Although I don't see why having a few people know about what I do matters. People know about you."

Jethro nodded. "Different rules for different ops."

"I'll just have to see how it shakes out, but I can't live a double life with Mercy. There's no way."

"It's going to be better this way. Your other choice is to walk away from Mercy, from Havoc . . . and you're too immersed to do that now."

"Is that what happened to you?"

"That's too long of a story for tonight."

"Ah, go ahead—we've got time," Vann said from the doorway between the kitchen and the living room.

"Is Vann supposed to know about all of this?" Linc asked.

"If I wasn't, it's too fuckin' late," Vann grumbled.

Linc couldn't help it—he laughed. Punch drunk, they called it, and now he understood exactly what the term meant. But he sobered quickly at the weight of what he was about to do, and exhaustion suddenly weighed him down. He stretched out on the couch, put his head on the pillow, and Jethro put a blanket on him. "I'm going from barely anyone knowing what I do to everyone knowing."

"Feels that way, but no, they won't. Just the ones who need to," Jethro assured him.

"Vann needed to?"

Vann sighed, obviously annoyed at being spoken about like he wasn't there.

"Vann and I knew each other another lifetime ago," Jethro continued.

"I really want to hear this," Linc murmured. "Wish I wasn't so tired."

Vann snorted. "It's not a fuckin' fairy tale."

"Don't crush my hopes and dreams," Linc instructed.

Jethro rolled his eyes and then got serious. "Here's the thing—you picked a job that basically ensured—and excused—your running."

"I enabled myself." Linc's head began to throb. He was surprised the adrenaline crash hadn't happened sooner.

Jethro nodded. "Nothing wrong with admitting you want something different now."

"And Hangmen is your something different?"

"I get to stay in one place," Jethro reasoned. "With what you're doing? Not so much."

"So I've got to make a choice."

"Or modify your current career path," Jethro agreed. "I'm sure Castle will help you work something out, if that's what you really want. Beyond that, there's plenty of things for you to do."

Linc chose to believe him.

CHAPTER 25

BE CAREFUL MAKING WISHES IN THE DARK

Linc chafed at the heavy restraints on his wrists. He couldn't move. *Fuck.* He shifted slightly, trying to stay small and quiet, because then they might forget about him for hours, might not hit him or drug him or fuck him, and thank fuck they always used condoms (for no other reason than they were worried about catching something *from him*.)

But the sudden weight on him, the hands touching him, would lead to yanking and hitting soon enough and no, he wasn't going into that open grave.

His leg shot out and made contact. He heard a muffled grunt and he punched, and then he charged like a bull at whoever had backed off momentarily. He made the tackle, his body falling on another man's hard as they hit the floor together, and then he searched blindly for the man's neck. Finally, he wrapped his hands around the man's throat and squeezed and the body under his bucked hard, forcing Linc to roll with him. He was conscious of yelling—his—and the sounds of a struggle. His body hurt, because he was slamming into walls and other objects that he couldn't place, but he wasn't giving up.

"Linc, baby, please . . ."

A voice broke through his consciousness, and who the fuck was calling him baby? No way—he wasn't falling for a trick.

He resumed his efforts to kill whoever was still goddamned grabbing at him, and further panic ensued when he realized it was more than one set of hands on him.

He went wild, throwing punches and kicks at the enemy Heathens he knew were there . . . until he finally heard, "Let him go—don't touch him." And then no one was touching him.

Still, he was restless, circling, seeing Bones and Bruno and the Heathens compound and that fucking room with the concrete floor with the chains attached and he snarled, "Stay the fuck back."

Bones held out his hands as if in surrender. "We're staying back."

"I'm getting out of here."

"You're out, Linc. You already escaped," Bones said, sounding too reasonable.

Yeah, this was definitely a trick. "You're not following me."

"Linc, come back. You're at Havoc. Safe. You're dreaming."

Of course he was dreaming—about Havoc and Mercy, but when he woke up it was always a lie.

"Linc, c'mon. It's Bram." *Bram?* No way. The Heathens hadn't captured Bram. But Bram was standing there, looking concerned. "Linc, you're bleeding."

"Of course I'm bleeding." Why were they all surprised? They'd done this to him, day after day and fuck.

"Linc, honey . . . I've got to examine you." A female voice. He blinked. He'd never heard a female voice the entire time he'd been held at Heathens. "It's Misha," she persisted.

Misha? What the hell? "You shouldn't be here. You've got to get out before they see you." He moved toward her, touched her and fuck, she smelled good, like sunshine.

She put her hand in his and whispered, "We'll go together." And then they walked through a door and into the night air, across a wooden porch until his bare feet hit grass, and he stared, unsure of where to go.

He heard panted breathing, realized it was his. Looked up and saw the moon high above the trees . . . and everything melted away except the cool night air caressing his skin, the moon, the trees, and Misha's hand in his.

Havoc.

"Fuck," he managed, his voice hoarse and raw sounding, even to his own ears. His knees threatened to give out and everything hurt. The disorientation had his head spinning, but he forced himself to stand there and breathe.

Misha gave his hand a light squeeze—encouragement and a reminder that he wasn't alone—all rolled into one.

"Fuck," he said again.

"Linc, there's a chair behind you. Come sit with me."

He turned and saw she was right, that two chairs had materialized behind them, and he sat shakily with her help, and then she sat, and still she held his hand.

"I grew up in this world," she started. "This rough and scary biker world. And I know people in med school used to wonder how I dealt with it. I was also asked if I was scared." She let out a short laugh that tinkled along the breeze. "I was raped, Linc—held down and raped in my own apartment by a blue blood who was in my study group. He was from a prominent family and he knew where I came from, and he told me that he figured biker chicks always wanted it."

Now, Linc was squeezing her hand as the world began to right itself rapidly. "Misha, I'm sorry."

"I get it, honey, and I didn't go through a quarter of what you went through. But when someone takes away all your control from you, it's always a fight to balance getting it back . . . letting yourself be helped and looked after. Talking about it helps too."

"Did Mercy come in and touch me?" he asked finally.

"I did." Mercy's voice came from somewhere behind him. "I needed to talk to you about what happened tonight so I shook your shoulder lightly to wake you. And you flipped."

Linc closed his eyes briefly as his mind raced backward. *Tonight . . . what happened tonight . . .*

Harry. Havoc teens. Project X. "You were pissed."

"A little, yes," Mercy said simply. "But more worried about you than anything. I remember what I agreed to last night. I'm not going back on my word."

Linc nodded, ashamed at how his body and brain had betrayed him. "Okay, it's okay," he told Mercy when really, he was the farthest thing from it.

"I have a sedative," Misha offered, because she knew. Linc figured they all knew how fucked up he was. Christ, the scene he'd made . . .

"Fuck no."

"Then you have to let me check you. I think you need stitches."

Linc nodded and stood, making sure his legs were under him. Mercy stayed close, and Vann and Jethro were on the porch, along with Sweet and Bram.

Bram followed them inside, where Tug and Boomer were, and sat next to him in the kitchen as Misha checked him, decided he didn't need stitches, and placed steri-strips on the cut above his eyebrow and his chin.

Mercy kept a hand on his shoulder the entire time. When Misha finished, she left with Boomer to go to Sweet's house.

"You still up for talking?" Mercy asked him quietly.

"Yes—I have to be." Linc looked around at the men who'd started to assemble—Sweet and Bram, Vann, Jethro, and Tug. "Let them stay. I mean, I wanted to tell you first, but in the interest of Havoc, it's better this way."

"Why don't you start by telling us about Luke Castle," Mercy said.

"He's an old Army friend. He's not in the Army anymore," Linc said carefully.

Bram and Sweet looked at each other. Tug sighed and Vann crossed his arms. And Mercy?

Looked too calm to be believed when he asked, "And what does non-Army Castle have you involved in?"

"He wasn't my handler when Heathens took me," Linc said. "He got rid of that guy."

"Were you on a job then, Linc?" Bram asked quietly and the room got tense.

"I was doing some recon, yes."

"And this is why your court case was closed chambers," Mercy added.

"How did you know? Ah fuck, never mind." Linc felt lighter now that his secret was out. He was also pretty sure that feeling wasn't going to last long.

"Who was in charge of your handler?" Bram's voice was low and reasonable.

It was his *I'm going to go out and kill someone with my bare hands for hurting my baby brother* voice. "Castle already took care of it," Linc reminded him.

"Was Castle in charge of your handler?" Bram repeated.

"You can't kill him, Bram."

"Oh, but I can. I can list all the fucking ways . . ." Bram started but Sweet put a hand on his chest.

"Bram, let's find out a little bit more and then you can flip the kill switch, all right?" Sweet raised his brows at Bram and Bram grunted in response.

Jethro sighed. "Not supposed to hear this shit, you know?"

Linc sank back into his chair. "Will all of you just calm the fuck down?" He was tired. Irritable. "In case you haven't notice, full grown-up over here."

"I've definitely noticed," Jethro told him.

Mercy bared his teeth and growled at him. Vann looked pleased at all the unrest.

Linc wondered if it was wrong that Mercy's jealousy warmed him. "Okay, look, one of our skips—Ty Larimer—had Blanchard for his attorney. It didn't seem right because how the hell could he afford a lawyer like that and why would Blanchard take a low-life thug on? He's a cartel lawyer. Ty missed court so I paid Blanchard a visit and before you say anything," he told Mercy, who'd opened his mouth but closed it now, "I didn't tell him who I was. I did get pictures of Ty's file. Castle told me the next day that Ty had been found murdered, cartel-style."

"Drugs?" Sweet asked.

Linc shook his head. "Human trafficking. Mainly teens."

Realization bloomed on the men's faces.

"Fuck," Vann muttered. "Those bastards got too close to our kids."

"I didn't want to take any chances tonight," Linc admitted. "After what happened last night, I just knew. With the Pagans trying to make their way into Shades . . . it's almost like they're running a distraction play."

"And Castle . . ." Bram drew out the man's name like a curse. "Wants you to work on this."

"Heathens can make you," Mercy pointed out tightly.

"I'd be dealing mainly with the cartel." Linc tried to not get annoyed and say something like, *Why didn't I think of that—you're right—the Heathens know me.*

"I think it's time for Linc and Mercy to talk alone," Sweet said, as if he noticed Linc's sudden tension toward Mercy. "We've got enough to talk about."

Bram pointed at his brother. "We need to talk more about this."

"Like we've talked about your career in the past?" Linc asked pleasantly. Bram took a step toward him but Sweet pulled him back, murmured something in his ear.

"Tomorrow, Linc," Bram called over his shoulder as Sweet led him out. Vann dipped his head before he left, following the others out the door and closing it behind them.

Linc turned to Mercy. "Here's the upshot—what I was going to tell you, and you alone tonight. I was running ops for Castle's guys when I was taken. After I woke in the hospital, he came to see me and I told him I was done. But after court, I told him that I'd start up again, because I wanted to make sure that what he told me about the cartel and the trafficking wasn't going to blow back on Havoc. And then those kids were way too goddamned close. I needed backup and I called Jethro, because Hangmen are closer and they're Havoc's allies. And I'm not supposed to tell anyone about this. No one. But your claiming shit threw a wrench in that."

He hadn't meant for it to come out in an angry tirade, but Mercy sat back under the force of Linc's words. "Fuck, baby, I just wanted you safe."

"Yeah, like I don't." Linc crossed his arms.

"I think I'm seeing the undercover agent come through," Mercy muttered. "Not sure I like it."

"You might have to get used to it if I decide to keep doing it. It's a part of me."

Mercy tilted his head. "The Jethro thing . . . it's because he understood the job, the risks."

"I think so. I mean, he lives it. But I'm sorry. I was just . . . flailing."

"No, babe, I'm sorry."

"Why? You were right. I wasn't ready—not all the way. And you were the only one I could tell everything to. The only one who needed to hear it as much as I needed to say it."

"I don't want to tie you down."

Linc gave him a smile that took over his whole face. "You're the only person I've ever wanted to do that with—in every sense of the word. Dig?"

Mercy snorted. "You'll be the death of me."

"But in a positive way, right?"

"Yeah, babe. Definitely. But here's what I don't get. You could've skated away from the bail responsibilities with no problem. Hell, you didn't even need to have any of it on your record. You didn't need the bond from me."

True, but Linc refused to admit that. But Mr. Dog-with-a-bone wasn't stopping.

"Why would you risk getting arrested?" he pressed.

"It was good for my cover," Linc said quickly.

"Bullshit."

"It's not." But it was only a partial truth.

The first time he'd seen Mercy, he'd been in Bertha's. Wearing the Havoc cut and watching Linc dance, the same look on his face that Ryker reserved for Rush.

But Ryker hadn't made Rush come to him. Not really. Ryker had shown up in Rush's bedroom, slowly seducing him into the idea of a relationship.

Mercy? He'd watched Linc with interest . . . but hadn't made a damned move. In order to get face time with him, Linc had to . . .

"Had to what?" Mercy asked.

Linc realized he'd muttered his story out fucking loud.

"What did you do to get my atten—" Mercy's eyes widened and he halted. "You got yourself arrested to get close to me."

Linc probably couldn't have felt stupider than he did right now. "I didn't . . . not exactly. I mean, I didn't plan it." It had been more of a split-second decision when he'd seen Mercy getting ready to leave alone, yet again. "You didn't want anything to do with me." Fuck, he was pathetic. "I got arrested because you wouldn't pay any attention to me any other way."

Mercy really stared at him now, noting Linc's blue eyes laid bare with honesty and truth. "I was paying attention to you. I just couldn't let you know. Jesus Christ . . . I knew that the second I touched you . . ."

Everything would explode. And it had.

And it hadn't stopped yet.

"Remember our first night?" Linc asked, almost shyly.

"I'll never fucking forget it," Mercy growled. "And, for the record, I did notice you . . . clocked you pretty much the second you started hanging around."

Linc scoffed. "That's when I was in the Army." Mercy stared at him, raised his brows and Linc couldn't hold back his surprise. "Really?"

"Are you kidding me? You really think I could ignore you?"

"You did a pretty good job of pretending," Linc said quietly. "I guess we both kept a lot of secrets."

"Are you telling me yours now because your back's against the wall?" Mercy had to ask.

"No. Check your texts."

Mercy scrolled and saw Linc's "Let's talk" text from eleven that morning. Then he frowned and scrolled back to a picture of a sunset that he'd never seen before. He and Linc hadn't spent any time texting, not for months. "Is this from tonight?"

Linc looked shaken. He took the phone from Mercy's hands and, finger on the screen, pushed the picture to the side to see the time and date. "Something must've happened . . . it never went through that day."

Mercy took the phone back because Linc's voice was hoarse with emotion. He saw that the date and time were just before Linc had been taken by the Heathens.

He'd been sending Mercy a picture of the sunset . . . with the words: *See you soon.*

"I wanted to share it with you," Linc murmured. "I was getting ready to turn around back to Havoc then."

It was like a hot knife through his heart. "I didn't see this, Linc. I . . ."

"They grabbed me right after . . . they probably turned my phone off so you couldn't trace it. I have no idea where that phone went. Someone must've turned it on recently or . . ." Linc shook his head. "I don't know."

Mercy brushed his knuckles across Linc's cheek. "I should've looked for you, Linc. No matter if I'd gotten this picture or not."

Linc gave a lopsided smile. "We're good, okay? You know now. That answers my question."

"And I just have one more—did you sleep with Castle?"

Linc rolled his eyes. "At one point in time, yes. Before I worked for him . . . and after, a little."

"Who broke it off with who?"

"I did." As Linc spoke those words, he stood and stripped off his T-shirt and threw it to the side, his cheeks slightly flushed, and looking more alive than Mercy had seen him in months.

Without speaking, Linc straddled his lap, winding his arms around Mercy's shoulders, bending his head to press his lips against Mercy's, and Mercy let Linc take the lead.

Then Linc unbuckled Mercy's belt and freed it, handing it over to Mercy. "I want you to tie me with this. And use me. And I don't want you to let me up, even if I beg. And I will beg."

Mercy stared at his boy's flushed face. "Yes, you will. I'll only stop if you say 'red.'"

In all their times together, Linc never had.

Linc's eyes grew serious. "Thank you."

"Let's get your pants off."

Linc moved away from him and skimmed his sweats off. Then Mercy took his belt and wound it around Linc's wrists, keeping his hands in front of him . . . and then he walked him around the back of the couch and put gentle pressure on his back so Linc bent over. His hands rested on the couch cushion, and he spread his legs apart and Mercy watched him do so without being told and Christ, the trust Linc gave him was incredible. A fucking gift, and one he'd never take for granted.

"You're mine, baby," he bent down to murmur in Linc's ear as his fingers searched out Linc's hole, rubbing, pressing, feeling Linc squirm back against him.

"Yes," Linc agreed.

"Claimed," he continued after he'd grabbed a bottle of lube and squirted it on his fingers, then resumed his fingering, using one, then two pressed inside of him.

"Yes." Linc's word was a half sob as Mercy added a third finger, then twisted and rubbed his gland. Linc went up on his toes and groaned. "More. I need more."

Mercy gave him more, but at his own speed. Pleasure rippled through Linc as he played . . . but it wasn't going to be enough and Mercy knew it. Kept edging him and then pulling back, until Linc was babbling about "needing to be fucked now."

Mercy chuckled, asked, "That's the spot, baby?" as he rubbed circles over his gland and Linc nodded. "Words."

"Yes, God, yes," Linc pleaded.

"You should see how hot you look—all splayed out for me. Half my hand in you and you're so fucking compliant. Letting me do whatever I want . . . letting me give you what you need."

A sob tore from Linc's throat, and it surprised him. It also made Mercy replace his fingers with his cock, pressing the thick head against his hole until Linc's body gave up and accepted him inside.

CHAPTER 26

LET ME SHOW YOU WHAT
I LEARNED OUT ON THE ROAD

The next morning, he woke to multiple voices, all talking intensely. He could make out Bram, Sweet, Mercy, Vann, Tug, and . . . Castle. *Shit.*

He got up, dressed, and padded downstairs, trying to get a read on what was happening.

That read came pretty quickly, because of all the yelling.

"I don't answer to any of you," Castle was telling the group calmly. "I'm here as a favor."

They all went silent when Linc walked in though.

"Listen, we're not going to do this *talk about Linc when he's not in the room* shit again, got it?" He scanned their faces and the men looked slightly chastened, except for Mercy.

"Did they call you?" Linc asked Castle now. "Because I didn't."

"I heard about what happened at the docks," Castle told him. "When I attempted to come in here, I had a mob waiting for me."

Linc fought a smile and glanced at Bram, because Sweet was literally standing between him and Castle. Vann, again, was enjoying the unrest and Mercy's hands were balled into fists. "The men in this room are the only ones who know right now. I need to tell Rush and Ryker and then I know my secret will be kept."

"It wasn't your goddamned secret to tell, Linc," Castle hissed, and Vann growled, a literal growl to rival any attack dog, and Castle shifted and stepped away from him. "I'm trying to protect you."

"Tried that," Mercy said. "It wasn't working for him. He's got to be able to tell us shit. We need to protect him and Havoc. It's the only way."

"Castle, not telling the men here—and maybe a few others—isn't going to work. That being said, if I decide to work with you on this job, that's not something anyone here can interfere with. I think you all need to know what Havoc's coming up against. We have a common enemy, and the faster we can get rid of them, the better."

Vann gave him a dip of his chin and Linc noted the approval. Bram and Mercy would, of course, be the hardest sells, but they remained quiet, for the moment at least.

"We need to talk now," Bram told him, right after Castle let himself out.

Linc figured there was no more avoiding it, so the two of them went out onto the back porch and waited, with Linc pretending to be completely innocent . . . because that sometimes worked with Bram.

But maybe not this time. Not when Bram demanded, "Do you have anything you'd like to tell me?"

"Um, I think you're the greatest older brother ever?" Linc said hopefully.

Bram rolled his eyes. "Something else?"

"And you're very handsome too. Oh, I know, you're a really great—"

"Linc!" Bram roared in a very familiar brother way that Linc had heard his entire childhood.

"I'm right here. You don't have to yell."

Bram's hands flexed. He'd never hit him, but he would make sure Linc didn't run from his questions. Linc backed up slightly, although he'd miscalculated the wall behind him.

"Linc, you never told me."

"Because you'd worry. And by the time it happened, you were already undercover."

"And when I got out of that first job—"

"I was already in and figured it was safer not to tell you."

"And you were right," Bram admitted defeatedly. "I didn't want this for you."

"What—a life of excitement and adventure?" Linc joked. "Most of the time, it's cool."

"And when it isn't?"

"When I have to lie to my family and friends, even if it's for their own good, I just tell myself that it's for the best."

"One of us needs a direct line to your handler," Bram instructed crisply.

"I already put it into your phone."

"When?"

"Half an hour ago."

"Linc—"

"You're really not mindful about—"

"You fucking pickpocket."

"I put it back!"

They looked at each other and then Linc snorted and so did Bram. Bram put a hand on his shoulder. "Yeah, I guess things are right back to where they should be."

"This is normal . . . for us."

Now that things were settled with Bram, Linc knew he had a bigger hurdle to overcome with Mercy. He steeled himself for their talk, and Bram gave him an encouraging pat on the back. There wasn't going to be an easy way to talk about this—and it was going to be in front of everyone, because all the men standing in Mercy's kitchen were now very much involved.

Mercy had obviously been waiting for him to come back inside. He didn't look angry, just tense and maybe even a little resigned to what he knew Linc would tell him.

Linc reiterated it anyway. He moved in close, to where Mercy leaned against the kitchen counters. "Hey."

"Hey." Mercy's hands went to his waist.

"You've got to let me do my job."

Mercy's expression tightened. "You need backup."

"I'll have it. Trust me. But Havoc can't be involved."

"We're not amateurs."

"I need to do this, Mercy. This is my job, and I'm good at it."

Mercy nodded slowly, acknowledging Linc's words. "It's how you survived at Heathens."

Linc nodded grimly. "That training, and thinking about you. Us. It was what I hung onto."

"But you knew it was my fault you were there."

"And what I'm telling you—what I've been trying to tell you for months—was that it didn't matter. Not then. Not now. You—us— that's what got me through."

"And I've been fucking it up ever since."

"No. Guilt is fucking you up—fucking *us* up and that's not what I want. I don't want to leave. But if I can't do this job—and this one's not only important to me, but to Shades—I'll have to. I want to help you—I want to do this for you. And for Havoc."

"How the fuck did all that wisdom get into someone so young?"

Linc rolled his eyes. "Okay, old man."

Mercy tugged him closer, then wrapped an arm around his waist. "Tell me how I can help. Because it will look worse if we aren't on our usual patrols."

"You'll make sure you get called away on some kind of wild-goose chase. So have someone create a diversion that would keep you and Havoc busy . . . and keep the kids at home."

"Before we do this . . . there's one more thing we need to settle." Mercy gave him a hard look and Linc knew exactly what he was talking about. He steered Linc closer to the group that waited—sans Castle—and said, "I know where David is buried."

Sweet frowned. The rest of the men looked slightly confused but didn't say anything.

"How?" Sweet asked.

Mercy looked at Linc. "I wish he didn't have to know about it . . . but they told him."

"Fuck," Sweet muttered.

"I'll show you where the grave is." He had to force himself not to say *graves*, because they'd see it soon enough.

"You can just tell me, Linc," Mercy started, but Linc shook his head.

"No. I need to go. You were right the other night—letting it out makes things better." And it had. He'd slept through last night, and while he wasn't expecting miracles, he was hopeful that he'd have more nights like that.

Mercy said, "If we bring him to his family . . ."

"There will be an investigation," Bram finished.

Mercy nodded. "Can't bring the body to them but I won't leave it there."

"I know," Sweet told him. "We won't. Let me talk to Post. I'm sure we can find a way." Post was a local funeral director. "Would you want to bury him on Havoc land? Wouldn't be the first."

"Would you do that?" Mercy asked, his voice halting.

"You're one of us. You claimed him at one time, which means he was also one of us. So yes, I would do that," Sweet told him.

Mercy looked at Linc. "I think David would've liked that."

CHAPTER 27

SOMEONE SAVED
MY LIFE TONIGHT

Linc got dressed the next morning, trying to ignore the nerves in his belly as he pushed the eggs Mercy made him around his plate.

He was going back to Heathens land, but he wasn't going to be alone. He'd be looking at the graves he still had nightmares about, but then it would be over. He'd be safe the whole time.

The doorbell rang, interrupting his thoughts.

"Can you grab that?" Mercy called.

Linc padded downstairs and saw Rush on the porch. He swallowed hard, not sure if he was ready for this face-to-face. Yes, they'd spoken on the phone when Rush had called to ask for his help . . . but that hadn't been the time or place to discuss their fight. And now, when Linc opened the door, it hung between them like a heavy curtain.

Linc leaned against the doorjamb and Rush didn't make a move to come in, just stared at him for a long moment. His voice was hoarse when he finally spoke. "You didn't tell me. Because you couldn't."

"Yes."

"Fuck, Linc." Rush ran his hands through his hair. "You were working. Since I knew you . . . since we got out . . . you weren't just hanging around, running off when you felt like it. It was your job. And I didn't know."

Linc's only answer was a shrug, because the knife Linc still had stuck in his heart hadn't dislodged.

Rush shook his head. "You let me think . . . you let me act like a total asshole to you."

"Seemed to come naturally," Linc told him and Rush's face dropped. "You only said what you think about me."

"C'mon, man, I was hurt and stupid. I was trying to get a rise out of you so you'd explain. I never thought . . . fuck. You're one of my best friends. I never want to hurt you."

"Rush—"

"I'm sorry. Fuck, Linc, all this time . . . if I'd known, you wouldn't have gone through what you did. I should've known—even if you didn't tell me, I should've known you better than to think you just ran." He finished with a small sob and hugged Linc, and for a second, Linc just stood there and let him. But Rush had stood by him, had worried about him.

"'S'all right," he told Rush as he put his arms around his friend.

Rush sniffled in his ear. "No, it's not. It didn't fit. You don't abandon your friends. I just want you to be happy and you seemed happy with Mercy and . . . I never thought . . ."

"I know." When Rush pulled back, Linc saw his eyes red. Linc's eyes were wet too. "I couldn't tell you. I still wasn't supposed to."

Rush nodded. "So Castle's your handler?"

"He is now. The guy before him is the one who fucked up by never reporting me."

Rush looked like he wanted to ask something but Linc knew exactly what it was. "And yes, I slept with Castle. But I didn't have to do it for the grades. He'd already recruited me. It was just a side bonus."

"How's Mercy feel about that?"

"He's not that happy."

"I'd imagine not. Then again, I know what happens when Ryker gets jealous so . . ."

Linc grinned. "Why don't you come inside and wait. Mercy's got *Grand Theft Auto.*"

Several hours later, two SUVs and a couple of bikes made the two-hour trip as Linc guided them to the spot that was just outside of the Heathens compound. Just far enough off their land so they couldn't get in trouble if the law discovered the graves.

Linc's gut clenched as they got closer, and he tried not to let the memories swamp him. But it was impossible. Even with Mercy's hand on his thigh and his friends surrounding him, this was going to be difficult.

Equally so for Mercy, Linc reminded himself. And that was the only reason he was doing this. For Mercy—so he could have the closure he deserved.

Vann was on his bike—riding in the truck was a rarity for him, Linc noticed. He much preferred his freedom. Linc could relate.

"Linc, you need to breathe," Mercy murmured against his cheek, and Linc nodded and closed his eyes as they drove past the burnt-out shell of the Heathens compound. It was hidden behind gates and up a long drive but still, Linc swore he could picture it as if it were right in front of him.

"Linc, we're past," Sweet told him. "Can you guide us from here?"

Linc opened his eyes and looked to the left. The field to the right was expansive and familiar. "Can you go straight here—slowly?"

Tug complied and Linc scanned the area until he caught sight of the tree, a large weeping willow that Linc recalled in some of his darker nightmares. "The tree." He swallowed hard.

Tug turned the big truck in the direction of the tree and drove past it . . . onto a dirt road.

"This is right," Linc murmured. "Keep going . . ."

After another half mile, Linc said, "Here. Stop here."

Another weeping willow. Beyond that, they'd find what they came for. Reluctantly, he got out of the truck and began walking woodenly over the land that he'd been led through time and time again during his capture, always with Bones at his back, always chained up and pushed along.

This was the root of most of his nightmares. And he was confronting it head-on.

For David. Because this could've been you.

Finally, he stopped ten feet from where he needed to be, and the men walking with him also stopped.

Mercy's arm went to his back and Linc wanted to turn tail and run. But he took one halting step after another, no one pressuring him until he stood at the spot where David was buried.

He refused to look to the right of the marker. But judging by the tension rolling off the men next to him, they all had.

"Jesus fuck . . . is that . . .?" Tug asked and then Vann's hand was on his shoulder. And finally, Linc glanced over and stared down at the open grave. The one the Heathens had dug just for him. The one they'd pushed him into, time and time again.

Bram turned away and choked back a sob, and Sweet went to him.

Rush turned his body into Ryker's and let the big man hold him.

Tug and Boomer and Shaman remained in stony silence, clearly upset.

Vann cursed softly. Linc stood between him and Mercy, who stared down at the grave, basically letting Linc hold him up . . . or hell, maybe Mercy was holding him up. It didn't matter, because they were both looking into the still open, empty grave and the one next to it, marked with a wooden white supremacist symbol.

Mercy growled and lunged, yanked it out of the ground and then crushed it under his boot. Linc put a hand on his shoulder and Mercy turned into him, bowed his head and cried silently on his shoulder.

"It's okay, Mercy. We'll get him out of here," Linc assured him. "Post is here."

"We're covering that other fucking grave," Mercy told him.

"I'm not arguing with that."

Vann touched Mercy's shoulder. "Let me help Post. You don't need to see him like this. You need to remember him in the good times, Mercy. I know you can do that."

Mercy glanced at Linc. "I can now."

Because putting David to rest was like putting an ending to Linc's captivity. The end of a horrible era . . . and the mission tomorrow was the promise of an entirely new—and better—one.

CHAPTER 28

UNDER PRESSURE

Over the next week, Linc met with Castle—and Mercy and Sweet and Bram as well, because Castle knew they'd be backing him up and helping with the op. It made the most sense, and kept Linc the safest, because Havoc's involvement would be seen as normal. If Havoc stood down, PX would know something was off.

But Linc was still the one taking the biggest risk, and he was okay with that. Because he'd been feeling better these last days. The nightmares were fading. Things between him and Mercy continued to get better—and while Linc knew he wasn't completely healed, he was well on his way.

And things on the dock had moved forward during this time as well. Linc resumed his role of Johnny O. and the cartel had done a few checks with his old Boston contacts and were satisfied that Johnny O.'s disappearance had been for work.

Castle had DEA and FBI resources ready to help bust the cartel's trafficking ring, and there was a plan. A timeline.

And then everything changed in a single instant, thanks to a call from Castle.

"Rumor has it that PX grabbed two girls off the street today. A warning to MCs to back off," Castle explained and a chill went up Linc's spine. "Is anyone missing?"

Linc checked the time. It was close to dinnertime, and the kids of Havoc knew they were still on lockdown and should be back by now. He'd need help to run bed checks. "I'll call you back," he told Castle and then called for Mercy, who came immediately.

"What's wrong?"

"I think PX took a girl—or girls—from Havoc."

Mercy kept a hand on Linc's shoulder and dialed Sweet, then Tug, and then they were in Mercy's truck as part of a grid search, a check in that went house by house.

"I'll take this one," Linc called as Mercy went left. The cabin he approached was a slightly larger version of Mercy's, which signaled family. Kids.

A woman who Linc had seen around the compound answered, saying, "I told you to take your house key with you," and Linc's heart sank. "Oh, sorry. It's Linc, right? I'm sorry—I thought you were my daughter. She's due home any minute."

"Can you call her? She's past curfew."

"Okay, sure," the woman said. "Come in and let me grab my phone. Should I call Daryl too?"

"Call your daughter first. Please," he said and she did.

"It's just going straight to voice mail. Is Julie in trouble for missing curfew?"

"Where was she going today?"

"She went to pick up her best friend—she lives at Hangmen's compound. They were going shopping. Let me try Annie's number." She dialed from her contacts and shook her head. "Voice mail."

Just then, Daryl came in. He was a Havoc MC member who worked at the garage on the compound and in town. "Linc? What's happening? I heard you guys were doing a search."

"I can't confirm just yet," Linc said numbly. "But two girls were taken off the street today by PX members. In retaliation to Havoc." The woman covered her mouth and Daryl looked stoic. "I need her car's make and model. License too."

"Of course."

"Can you call Boomer with it? He's out looking for abandoned cars now. It happened by the docks," Linc said. "I'm sorry. If it is Julie, we'll get her back. Just like they got me back."

That seemed to soothe the woman. She reached out and touched Linc's shoulder. "That's the most reassuring thing I can hear right now."

Linc went out onto the porch of the Norse home when Sweet arrived to talk to Julie's parents. He put a hand on Linc's shoulder and squeezed as he walked by, and Linc warmed inside at the approval.

Now, he had to call Jethro and break the news to him.

"What's up? I heard from Castle about the missing girls," Jethro said. "We didn't want to freak everyone out since you were already checking things out on your end."

It had only been twenty minutes since Castle's phone call. "There's a girl missing from Havoc," he told Jethro now. "Julie Norse. She's friends with Annie Morrison." And Annie Morrison was the daughter of a Hangmen.

Jethro cursed. "Hold on." He heard Jethro calling out and voices in the background. "Linc, Annie's MIA. Where were they?"

"Headed to the mall. Julie was driving, and Boomer's out looking for her car."

Jethro paused. "So we're moving the timeline up?"

"Yes."

"Clue me in after you talk to Castle. We've got backup, but I'm going to try to convince these guys not to make things worse."

"Yeah, good luck with that." Because Linc was going to have similar trouble.

Half an hour later, they regrouped in the clubhouse. Jethro was there too.

"Where did Heathens relocate to?" Sweet asked.

"An hour north of the docks," Mercy confirmed. "There's an old warehouse district with several deserted buildings that they've taken over—with the help of Project X. PX is sniffing around, putting out feelers to the Heathens who are left."

Sweet considered this. "We can wait and hope they push south . . . or we can go in and try to drive them out."

"Pagans still on their side?" Tug asked.

"Undetermined. They're not our friends, but they're not looking to go to war with us—or Hangmen either." Mercy was finding it hard to sit still and just talk. He wanted the sun to rise on some Heathen bodies, but he was willing to let Sweet guide Havoc the way he always had.

"Vipers?" Vann broke in.

"At our backs, always," Sweet confirmed. "Just spoke to Cage last night."

Linc came in with a knock. Technically, he had no place in church, but Sweet granted him a special dispensation for this.

He went over to where Mercy sat and stood next to him, which made Mercy smile, even if he did try to hide it. "You got news, Linc?"

Linc nodded. "I spoke with Castle. He's concerned that retaliation against Project X could trigger the cartel. They don't want to lose their pipeline, and that's not a war Havoc wants."

"So what's the play then?" Mercy bit out, irritated by the mere mention of Castle's name.

Linc remained calm. "First, we need to get the girls back. I can do that. I'll take Vann as my driver, and if that goes well, I can break that open without ruining my cover."

"And then we blow the fuck out of PX?" Vann asked hopefully. "I've got extra C4 I've been saving for a special occasion."

Sweet glanced over at Vann, frowning. Tug was trying not to laugh and Vann looked completely serious. Because, as Mercy knew, he was.

As satisfying as it would be for Linc to watch Vann blow the fuck out of the PX (and maybe even join in to help), that probably wouldn't help the plan run as smoothly as Castle would like.

"We might not have to," he said. "If I can pull it off, I should be able to make the cartel think that PX sold them out. The cartel will turn on PX, and I have a feeling the cartel will come out on top."

"Love to get rid of both, but one problem at a time." Sweet nodded at Linc. "Time's of the essence, no?"

"Definitely. I'm ready to move out in a couple of hours. Castle's put out feelers and I should be able to broker a deal for the container that they're holding the girls in."

"So they're not hurt?" Boomer asked.

"Not yet," Linc said. "But we can't let that container leave the docks. The missing girls are in there."

"You think they'd be that stupid?"

"There's no place else for them to keep them—they need to get rid of the evidence. There's no better way for them to do that than to ship them out of the country, never to be seen again," Linc reasoned and Tug blanched.

"Those fuckers," he muttered. "I'd like to kill them."

"One thing at a time," Sweet told him. "First, the girls. Then we take our revenge. And we'll have plenty of help."

Through it all, Mercy was quiet, watching Linc carefully. But he didn't look concerned. No, he looked . . . proud. And it made Linc warm inside, the amount of trust Mercy was placing on him.

He'd make sure he didn't let Mercy—or Havoc—down.

CHAPTER 29

THE WILD BOYS ARE CALLING

Several hours later, the takedown was put in motion. Castle had okayed the resources, and even if he hadn't, Linc would've just gone ahead. Time was critical.

Linc had been inside himself most of the day, going over the plan silently, thinking of all the different scenarios that could happen. Preparing for them. Mercy had stayed close, letting him run scenarios by him, helping him map out locations, and just listening to him.

Finally, he grabbed Mercy's hand. "Is this hard for you?"

"Helping you? No. Getting you ready for battle? Yes. Doesn't matter that you're trained. I'm always going to wish I could step in and protect you. I imagine you feel the same about me."

"You know I do, Mercy." He looked into Mercy's eyes. "We've come a long way."

Mercy smiled. "Not always easy, but worth it."

"Very." He leaned forward and kissed Mercy, a slow kiss that warmed immediately. He brushed more kisses along Mercy's jaw, letting the rough stubble scratch him. "I love you, Mercy. I think I have for longer than I realized."

Mercy pulled back then to stare into his eyes. "I love you too, baby. And I'm there with you, tonight. Backing you up, however you need me to. Now go. I think Vann's waiting for you."

Linc glanced over his shoulder only once at Mercy, who sat with Sweet, Bram, and Ryker. They were all geared up, had weapons, and they'd follow far enough behind Linc and Vann so they wouldn't be seen. Rush and Noah were at Bertha's, getting the back room cleared out as a triage for the rescued girls. Tug, Boomer, and some of the other men were already heading to the docks from Bertha's. Hangmen were at the ready, as were Vipers, waiting with the Hangmen at their compound. For now, the rollout would be small, but everyone was on alert, in case anything bigger was necessary.

Linc just prayed his cover as Johnny O. continued to hold up at the docks. So far, he'd met with the man representing the cartel twice this week, assuring him that customs inspections wouldn't be an issue. The shipment was due to leave the docks that day, and Johnny O. needed to be there to ensure things went smoothly.

He had weapons. Men in place. It all came down to timing, and praying that no one got suspicious.

Castle had texted him twenty minutes ago, assuring him that the heavily guarded container was still at the docks. If they'd tried to move it earlier, that would've necessitated a shoot-out that could've endangered the girls inside the container. And Linc was relatively sure that the two MC girls weren't the only victims inside.

Now, they were ten minutes out. Vann was driving Linc, posing as Linc's bodyguard-slash-driver, his muscle, as it were, since very few people knew Vann at all. He'd done that for the first two meetings, so the cartel wouldn't be suspicious at seeing him now.

"You ready?" Linc asked from where he sat behind the darkly tinted windows of Vann's imposing ride. "And if you say that you were born ready . . ."

"But I was," Vann told him seriously.

Linc snorted. "Remember—"

"You're Johnny. I'm Vance." Vann knew his shit. He'd almost morphed into a different person by the time they reached the docks, the way he'd done the last two times.

Then again, so had Linc. "I want to know about you and Jethro."

"Is now really the time to ask that?"

"Yes."

Vann stared straight ahead. "I tried to kill him once."

"Like, seriously? Or in a bar fight?"

Vann shrugged. "Like, seriously. Not in a bar fight. He's got a scar from it."

"Vann?"

"What? I don't regret it—he deserved it. And he tried to kill me back. *And* I've got a scar," Vann added the last part like that excused all of it.

"So you guys were flirting."

"Fuck you, Linc," Vann grumbled and Linc snorted. He felt looser. More ready to take this on. He needed that break in the kill thoughts running through his mind.

Now, as they pulled into the dock area, he got a text that their men were in position near the container. They would be responsible for freeing whoever was inside, quietly, with help from customs.

Once the cartel happened on the empty container? Well, Linc just hoped the plan worked without any innocent bloodshed.

"Explosives are in place," Vann said before he got out. "You've got this."

Linc nodded and let himself out, walked toward the two customs agents waiting, who were really undercover agents and Castle's operatives. He let the cartel watch him, looking at their manifests, talking with them, pointing over to the container and Rios, the man in charge.

Finally, one of the undercover agents walked toward the cartel guards. "Your container's cleared. You guys have to back away so we can get it loaded."

"We need to stay with it. Part of the deal."

"The deal was not having it checked. Count your goddamned blessings. I'm in charge from here on out," Linc-as-Johnny O. told them.

Rios narrowed his eyes. "This was not explained."

"It was. To you and your boss. Unless you want to call this whole deal off, but I have to maintain relationships here." Linc stood firm on that. To back down now and show weakness would not work at all.

Finally, after a phone call, Rios relented. "My men will go. But you and I will remain with the container."

"Fair enough." Linc nodded at the agent, who grumbled about rules but ultimately waved to the other man, as if to say "all good."

"Are you going to need help on the return trip?" Linc asked Rios when the agent walked away.

"Possibly. But if this goes well, we have another container ready to go out of the country in two days."

Shit. Two days, another container. How many victims were they collecting? He'd have to find the warehouse after this. And how would that work?

Put this container on the ship. Empty. And then get the next container moving faster. It was the only way. It would take two days for them to realize the container was empty.

They'd have to empty the container on the ship. He glanced at Vann, who gave him the barest of nods. He knew too. Somehow, he'd signal Sweet and Mercy and the agents as well.

For now, Linc forced himself to stand there and watch the container get loaded.

Mercy got a text from Vann. *Unload on the ship. No other way. More vics.*

"Shit," he muttered.

"We need a distraction," Sweet said. "Keep Rios and the others from seeing us unload."

"We'll take care of that." Jethro pointed between himself and Bram, then texted Linc and Vann, *When you hear the boom, get them running.*

From where he, Sweet, and Ryker were hiding, they could easily get onto the ship without being seen. They walked through the already unloaded containers and found the one they needed. One of the undercover agents helped them open it up and Mercy stared inside, unable to move.

The girls they'd been looking for were there, along with maybe twenty others. All of them were chained to the walls of the container. They were filthy. Crying.

Alive.

"Jesus Christ," Sweet muttered as Mercy moved forward, reassuring the girls that they were okay. The MC girls were amazingly resilient, assuring the others that they knew them, that they would help them to safety.

"C'mon, honey," Mercy urged one of the girls, but she looked bad. Dehydrated for sure and unable to walk.

"We're lined up and ready to go," Ryker told him.

Mercy leaned down and picked her up. "I've got you. We're going to get you out of here."

"Boomer's got a van—we'll put them in there for now and sort it out at Bertha's."

"Going to need Misha," Mercy said quietly.

Several tense moments later, the boom they'd been waiting for happened along the west sides of the dock. "Let's roll," he barked, and said a silent prayer that this was going to go in their favor.

When the explosion went off, Rios automatically ducked and rolled. Granted, so did Linc and Vann, which probably gave them more credibility than anything.

"What happened?" Rios demanded.

"I was standing next to you when it happened," Linc reminded him. "All I know is it didn't happen on the ship. And I don't plan on hanging around to find out what it was."

"Ship's pulling away," Vann told them. "So should we." He motioned for Linc to follow him. "Rios, I'll get you to the lot safely."

Rios surprisingly agreed to walk with them. Linc didn't see the Havoc van in the lot and he hoped that meant things worked out.

"Tell me about the next shipment," Linc said.

"I'll be in touch."

"No way—you're giving me too short a lead time. I've got to let my guys know today if you've got a container coming in here within forty-eight hours."

Rios frowned. "Same size. Same merchandize. We'll be in contact tomorrow."

Linc nodded and made a show of walking toward the agents as Rios pulled away.

Vann said, "I planted a tracker on the car. They won't find it." He checked his phone. "We're going to have to wait until he stops moving. Then I have to turn it off while they scan the car. They do that shit."

"I guarantee the warehouse is close to the docks—they wouldn't risk a long haul," Linc said.

"Think you're right." Vann was staring at his phone. "Tracker's off." He showed Linc the coordinates and the map, which pinpointed Rios's car at a warehouse four blocks away.

"Make sure he doesn't move." Linc called Mercy, who answered on the first ring.

"You good, babe?" Mercy asked.

"We're clear for now," Linc said. "The girls?"

"Twenty in all. One of them's critical—she's a runaway. Misha's on the way to the hospital with her. We're keeping the girls here until nighttime, and then we'll transport them quietly."

"Vann, Jethro and I have to go get the other girls," Linc said as he saw Jethro and Bram walking toward them, grinning ear to ear, obviously pleased with themselves about the explosion. "We've got to do it now."

"Castle?"

"I'm sure he'll send backup."

"So will we, Linc. Let me know the location," Mercy said firmly, and Linc told him. "I'll meet you there."

Linc didn't bother to argue this time.

"Nice distraction," Vann was telling Bram and Jethro. "Mine would've been bigger."

Jethro rolled his eyes. Bram shot him the finger and asked, "Where's the other container?"

"They're at the warehouse—the abandoned one, close to Bertha's," Vann confirmed.

Jethro looked tense. "Going to be heavily guarded by PX."

"Fuck." Vann ran a hand through his hair.

"What the hell did you blow up?" Linc asked.

"We threw some C4 around that Bram had in his pocket," Jethro said and Bram shrugged like C4 in his pocket was a normal occurrence. "I'm sure we'll catch shit from it, but it was the best we could do under short notice. You call Castle?"

Linc was doing that as Jethro spoke. As soon as Castle picked up, Linc told him, "There are more vics at the warehouse where the PX have been squatting."

Castle sighed. "You go and you'll blow your cover."

"Then I'll make sure no one sees me," Linc shot back. Bram was watching him, shaking his head but not actually saying no. He knew he was taking a chance, but hell, that was part of his job. Either he was all in, or he was done, here and now. And this wasn't how he wanted to end his job. "I've got to see this through, Bram."

"I know you do. But you'll have to get the girls out. You can't show your face and you know that."

Jethro handed him a bandana to wrap his hair in and he also gave Linc his cut. Vann handed over his sunglasses. "Keep those on until you're in the container. And take them off only if you can't see. Anyone who sees you? Kill them," Jethro told him in no uncertain terms. "You can't leave anyone alive who sees you."

"Got it. Let's go."

The ride to the warehouse was quick. They parked around the corner and went in as dusk fell. The men were partying, oblivious to the fact that things hadn't gone their way that day. Linc saw the container, unattended, the door cracked. He motioned that he was going in and suddenly, Mercy was at his back, following him in.

Once in, he saw the girls chained against the sides of the container. They shrank back, fearing that he'd hurt them. He put his hand up, went to each one of them on the left side telling them they were safe, releasing them but telling them to stay put. Mercy did the same going down the right side of the container.

They heard the shouts, shots, mini-explosions and they waited until they had a clear yet smoky path out to the street. Finally, Linc gave the word and Mercy led the women out, with Linc taking the rear.

Suddenly, he was slammed against the side of his head. He caught himself, but a strong arm grabbed him and laughed. "You're Mercy's bitch. Nice to see you again."

Linc didn't hesitate—he recognized the Heathen from being locked in their goddamned basement, and he grabbed the knife he had on him and jammed it into the man's carotid. The man's mouth opened, he looked stunned, and then he dropped, shaking as blood pooled around him. Linc took the knife out and waited until he didn't feel a pulse before dragging him into the container and locking him inside.

No witnesses. And no, there wasn't a damned bit of guilt felt.

And when he went to the street, Jethro took the vest and the bandanna, hustling him into an FBI agent's car and telling him to play along.

"You did good, kid," Jethro told him. "You're safe. See you on the other side."

CHAPTER 30

ON THEIR WAY BACK
FROM THE FIRE

The other side turned out to be Bertha's by way of the FBI through the police station.

Linc was shaky after all was said and done. Too many memories, and even with the victory, it was all coming at him a little too hard and too fast.

They'd managed to keep his face away from the cartel and PX, so his cover wasn't blown. But hell, whether he wanted to keep doing this shit with Castle was still up in the air.

"Don't think about it tonight," Jethro warned him. "You did a lot of good. You still can, whether or not you stick with Castle."

Linc had nodded and wrapped the blanket more tightly around him. They'd ended up in Bertha's back room, where emergency services were helping the girls, thanks to Misha. Outside, it looked like business as usual, because the club was still open to avoid suspicion.

Now, he leaned against the wall, drinking a coke. Misha had checked him out and deemed him fine, but in need of rest, so of course Mercy was watching him like a hawk.

For once, he didn't mind it so much. Realized he needed it, especially when Mercy touched his shoulder from behind and he jumped. Fuck. "Shit. Sorry. I'm still hyped up."

"'S'all right, baby. Gonna make it all better. Taking you home now," Mercy murmured against his cheek.

Linc wanted the contact but knew he might freak a little. With Mercy? He could manage it. Even the nightmares, because waking up next to Mercy made everything better. "I want to make sure—"

"Home. Now. This is handled."

As of now, the cartel had no idea that the container was arriving empty. The men who'd been at the warehouse, including Rios, were arrested. And they'd made sure that Rios saw Linc at the police station, in cuffs, and angry, yelling for his lawyer.

So yeah, Johnny O. was still in the clear. The police made sure to inform Rios that Johnny O. refused to talk and was headed to prison. The girls were being taken care of—and there were no casualties on the sides of Havoc, Hangmen, Vipers, and Castle's men.

Based on all that, Linc saw zero point in arguing, so he let Mercy lead him out of the clubhouse and he got onto the back of Mercy's bike and wrapped around him for the ride home. Because, at least for tonight, they had the freedom of having no escorts. It was just the two of them.

Finally.

"Take the long way," Linc murmured, probably too low for Mercy to hear but somehow he did. And even after the ride down the highway that vibrated between Linc's legs and drove him crazy, he also took a ride around the compound, not leisurely but not fast either. It was perfect, all that revving engine between Linc's legs as he clung to Mercy's broad chest, his face in the wind and freedom at his back.

After what seemed like forever, Mercy pulled up to his cabin and parked. Linc hopped off and then Mercy dismounted and turned to look at him with a heat in his eyes that Linc could see even with only the dim porch light.

"Yeah," Linc said in response. "C'mon, Mercy. Please. Order me around. Please. Make me do things. Don't let me think. And don't let me up . . . not until I come hard enough to stop the wheels from spinning."

"You didn't even have to ask. Because I've been planning how I'm going to tie you down all night. I'm going to frustrate you. Make you beg. Scream. Squirm."

Linc was already doing the latter, just from the sound of Mercy's voice, dulcet and rough, graveled Southern drawl all mixed together. He started stripping as he walked in the door, leaving his clothes in a trail, was about to bend over to take his boots off until Mercy came up behind him and stopped him. Turned him. Picked him up and forced Linc to wrap around him, his jean-clad cock rubbing against Mercy's, frustrated as hell.

Mercy kissed him, teased his tongue against Linc's before fisting his hand in Linc's hair to deepen the kiss. He placed Linc on the kitchen table, continuing to kiss him while Linc brought his leg up and unlaced his boots and managed to kick them off one by one, even while being held in place.

Mercy chuckled against his mouth. If there was one thing about Linc, he was goddamned resourceful, and it was fun to watch him when he needed this badly. He was a brat when it came to shit like this, and Mercy didn't mind a damned bit.

Now that he had his boy naked against him, he didn't want to let him go for anything. It was with great reluctance that he walked him upstairs, put him on his knees, and made him wait while he found nipple clamps.

Linc looked between them and Mercy and frowned. "You've never . . ."

"It's about time I did. Maybe I'll end up piercing you, but until that happens . . ." He trailed off as he grabbed one of Linc's nipples between his thumb and forefinger, rolled it until it was taut and Linc was groaning, and then he placed the tight clamp on it. Linc hissed in a breath and then a smile hit his face. "Yeah, knew you'd love that."

He repeated the action with Linc's other nipple with the same reaction.

"Take my cock out," he instructed Linc next. "You haven't been paying enough attention to it lately."

Linc's smile went wide as he did what Mercy asked of him, freeing Mercy's cock, then licking along the length of the underside before taking it in his mouth. Mercy tugged at his hair, fucking his face after several moments of letting Linc get used to him and yeah, his dick in Linc's mouth with Linc's nipples clamped and fuck, that looked good. Really fucking good. He stroked a hand through Linc's hair and Linc looked up at him, his eyes nearly translucent with want and need and pure, unadulterated pleasure.

It was always urgent between them, with or without the danger. Didn't matter if this happened out of love or anger or frustration. It all mixed together to form the perfect balance for them. They were well aligned, in bed and in life.

Linc tried to make Mercy come in his mouth, and even when Mercy attempted to pull away, Linc refused to give in and finally, he got his reward. Mercy shot into his mouth with a groan and a curse and Linc happily drank him all down.

"You're going to pay for that."

"I hope so," Linc murmured, his voice hoarse from Mercy face-fucking him.

"Hands and knees, on the bed," Mercy told him, helped him up, because he'd been on his knees for a while, and he was already light-headed from the stimulation. "Spread your legs more. Good boy."

Linc blushed as Mercy's hand stroked his ass, his cock, brushed his already far too sensitive nipples. "Beautiful. God, I'd love to take you to the downtown and let total strangers watch you. Maybe I'll spank you right out in the open, make you walk over to me in front of everyone and lay across my lap and ask me to spank you."

"Mercy." Linc groaned his name like a prayer.

"You'd like that, I know. Fuck, you're blushing, even now." Mercy's hand stroked along Linc's ass cheeks and Linc squirmed, anticipation making his nerves jolt, because he wanted Mercy to spank him, to make him cry out in pain and pleasure until he'd spent everything inside, good and bad.

Finally, Mercy's hand came down on his ass, hard and fast, two slaps at a time on each cheek with no rest in between, until Linc was flying, yelling, unable to keep still. And just when he thought he couldn't take it, he started to come. Mercy reached under his body and took the clamps off, which drew out his orgasm to an almost unbearable length, and he lay there, face against the mattress and ass in the air, groaning. Mercy slid a hand along his belly and slicked his cock with Linc's come. And when Mercy's cock entered him, hard, fast and raw, Linc swore he'd come again on the spot. He pushed back against Mercy's cock, until Mercy pulled out and turned him, forcing

Linc to sit on his lap and ride him while Mercy leaned against the headboard.

Linc wrapped his arms around Mercy, buried his face against Mercy's hair, his cheek, murmured, "Falling in love with you was like falling out of the sky."

"Won't let you hit the ground, baby. Love you."

"You're mine, Mercy," he panted. "All fucking mine. You might've claimed me, but I claimed you right back."

His body strained, tugging him to orgasm, pushed off the cliff . . . falling out of the sky.

"Won't let you hit the ground, baby."

No, Mercy never would.

CHAPTER 31

JUST A SONG BEFORE I GO

Although they'd pulled off a successfully rescue and drove most of the PX out of Shades and the surrounding area for now, Havoc needed to maintain a constant, enforcing presence. Havoc would have help with that—along with Vipers and Hangmen, they'd keep a constant watch out. Sweet talked about asking the Lo Riders or the Skulls to come bring a chapter closer to Shades, and maybe Sons of Bastards too. There was definitely room for a neutral MC to move to a nearby town and build a compound . . . a club willing to be independent but wanting to help out.

Linc was still working for Castle, but only in the immediate area. With Bram and Jethro, there was constant intel-gathering and Mercy didn't have to worry as much.

But hell, who was he kidding—he'd always worry. And when Linc wasn't working for Castle, he and Mercy still ran the bail bonds shop, together. Because, as Linc pointed out, if it hadn't been for that shop, they might not have gotten together.

"I figure you'd have found a way," Mercy told him, but he understood the sentiment. And, with Linc's urging, they took on bigger cases, and they'd ended up going on chases together. They even discussed franchising.

Bram patched in with Havoc and stayed with the ATF, moving over to Jethro's team, and he got a new handler. Linc wasn't sure if he wanted to patch in, but Mercy was fine with that—because Linc was one of them, patch or no patch.

And Linc was his. *Always.*

So yes, things were settled on that front . . . but for Havoc, Mercy couldn't help but feel like the chaos was just beginning.

Explore more of the *Havoc Motorcycle Club* series:
riptidepublishing.com/collections/series-havoc

Dear Reader,

Thank you for reading SE Jakes's *Running on Empty*!

We know your time is precious and you have many, many entertainment options, so it means a lot that you've chosen to spend your time reading. We really hope you enjoyed it.

We'd be honored if you'd consider posting a review—good or bad—on sites like **Amazon, Barnes & Noble, Kobo, Goodreads, Twitter, Facebook, Tumblr,** and your blog or website. We'd also be honored if you told your friends and family about this book. Word of mouth is a book's lifeblood!

For more information on upcoming releases, author interviews, blog tours, contests, giveaways, and more, please sign up for our weekly, spam-free newsletter and visit us around the web:

Newsletter: riptidepublishing.com/newsletter
Twitter: twitter.com/RiptideBooks
Facebook: facebook.com/RiptidePublishing
Goodreads: tinyurl.com/RiptideOnGoodreads
Tumblr: riptidepublishing.tumblr.com

Thank you so much for Reading the Rainbow!

RiptidePublishing.com

ALSO BY SE JAKES

Havoc Motorcycle Club
Running Wild
Running Blind

Hell or High Water (EE, Ltd.)
Catch a Ghost
Long Time Gone
Daylight Again
Not Fade Away
If I Ever

Men of Honor
Bound by Honor
Bound by Law
Ties That Bind
Bound by Danger
Bound for Keeps (EE, Ltd.)
Bound to Break

Phoenix, Inc.
No Boundaries

Standalone
Free Falling (EE, Ltd.)
Sinners

Dirty Deeds (EE, Ltd.)
Dirty Deeds
Dirty Lies (Coming soon)
Dirty Love (Coming soon)

Inked
Hold The Line
Thirds

ABOUT THE AUTHOR

SE Jakes writes m/m romance. She believes in happy endings and fighting for what you want in both fiction and real life. She lives in New York with her family and most days, she can be found happily writing (in bed). No really . . .

SE Jakes is the pen name of *New York Times* best-selling author Stephanie Tyler (and half of Sydney Croft).

You can contact her the following ways:

Email: authorsejakes@gmail.com

Instagram: instagram.com/authorstephanietyler

Website: sejakes.com

Tumblr: sejakes.tumblr.com

Facebook: Facebook.com/SEJakes

Twitter: Twitter.com/authorsejakes

Goodreads Group: Ask SE Jakes

Truth be told, the best way to contact her is by email or in blog comments. She spends most of her time writing but she loves to hear from readers!

Enjoy more stories like
Running on Empty
at RiptidePublishing.com!

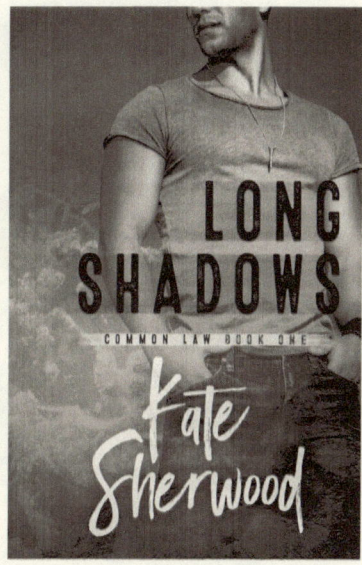

Watch Point   *Long Shadows*

What happens when the sexy   Sometimes a bad decision is so
fantasy turns into scary reality?   much better than a good one.

ISBN: 978-1-62649-674-3   ISBN: 978-1-62649-526-5